George Cary Eggleston

**A Man of Honor**

George Cary Eggleston

**A Man of Honor**

ISBN/EAN: 9783743303300

Manufactured in Europe, USA, Canada, Australia, Japa

Cover: Foto ©Andreas Hilbeck / pixelio.de

Manufactured and distributed by brebook publishing software
(www.brebook.com)

George Cary Eggleston

# A Man of Honor

"I'VE GOT YOU NOW."

(Frontispiece. See page 108.)

# A MAN OF HONOR.

BY

## GEORGE CARY EGGLESTON.

ILLUSTRATED.

NEW YORK:

ORANGE JUDD COMPANY,

245 BROADWAY.

*TO MARION, MY WIFE.*

# PREFACE.

I have long been curious to know whether or not I could write a pretty good story, and now that the publishers are about to send the usual press copies of this book to the critics I am in a fair way to have my curiosity on that point satisfied.

# CONTENTS.

9

# ILLUSTRATIONS.

### BY M. WOOLF.

# A MAN OF HONOR.

## CHAPTER I.

*Mr. Pagebrook gets up and calls an Ancient Lawgiver.*

MR. ROBERT PAGEBROOK was "blue." There was no denying the fact, and for the first time in his life he admitted it as he lay abed one September morning with his hands locked over the top of his head, while his shapely and muscular body was stretched at lazy length under a scanty covering of sheet. He was snappish too, as his faithful serving man had discovered upon knocking half an hour ago for entrance, and receiving a rather pointed and wholly unreasonable injunction to "go about his business," his sole business lying just then within the precincts of Mr. Robert Pagebrook's room, to which he was thus denied admittance. The old servant had obeyed to the best of his ability, going not about his business but away from it, wonder-

11

ing meanwhile what had come over the young gentleman, whom he had never found moody before.

It was clear that Mr. Robert Pagebrook's reflections
were anything but pleasant as he lay there thinking,
thinking, thinking—resolving not to think and straightway thinking again harder than ever. His disturbance
was due to a combination of causes. His muddy boots
were in full view for one thing, and he was painfully conscious that they were not likely to get themselves blacked
now that he had driven old Moses away. This reminded
him that he had showed temper when Moses's meek knock
had disturbed him, and to show temper without proper
cause he deemed a weakness. Weaknesses were his pet
aversion. Weakness found little toleration with him,
particularly when the weakness showed itself in his own
person, out of which he had been all his life chastising
such infirmities. His petulance with Moses, therefore,
contributed to his annoyance, becoming an additional
cause of that from which it came as an effect.

Our young gentleman acknowledged, as I have already
said, that he was out of spirits, and in the very act of
acknowledging it he contemned himself because of it.
His sturdy manhood rebelled against its own weakness,
and mocked at it, which certainly was not a very good
way to cure it. He denied that there was any good
excuse for his depression, and scourged himself, mentally,
for giving way to it, a process which naturally enough
made him give way to it all the more. It depressed him
to know that he was weak enough to be depressed. To
my thinking he did himself very great injustice. He

"MR. ROBERT PAGEBROOK WAS 'BLUE.'"

was, in fact, very unreasonable with himself, and deserved to suffer the consequences. I say this frankly, being the chronicler of this young man's doings and not his apologist by any means. He certainly had good reason to be gloomy, inasmuch as he had two rather troublesome things on his hands, namely, a young man without a situation and a disappointment in love, or fancy, which is often mistaken for love. A circumstance which made the matter worse was that the young man without a situation for whose future Mr. Robert Pagebrook had to provide was Mr. Robert Pagebrook himself. This alone would not have troubled him greatly if it had not been for his other trouble; for the great hulking fellow who lay there with his hands clasped over his head "cogitating," as he would have phrased it, had too much physical force, too much of good health and consequent animal spirits, to distrust either the future or his own ability to cope with whatever difficulties it might bring with it. To men with broad chests and great brawny legs and arms like his the future has a very promising way of presenting itself. Besides, our young man knew himself well furnished for a fight with the world. He knew very well how to take care of himself. He had done farm labor as a boy during the long summer vacations, a task set him by his Virginian father, who had carried a brilliant intellect in a frail body to a western state, where he had married and died, leaving his widow this one son, for whom in his own weakness he desired nothing so much as physical strength and bodily health. The boy had grown into a sturdy youth when the mother died, leaving

him with little in the way of earthly possessions except
well-knit limbs, a clear, strong, active mind, and an
independent, self-reliant spirit.    With these he had
managed to work his way through college, turning his
hand to anything which would help to provide him with
the necessary means—keeping books, "coaching" other
students, canvassing for various things, and doing work
of other sorts, caring little whether it was dignified or
undignified provided it was honest and promised the
desired pecuniary return.    After graduation he had
accepted a tutorship in the college wherein he had stud-
ied—a position which he had resigned (about a year
before the time at which we find him in a fit of the
blues) to take upon himself the duties of "Professor of
English Language and Literature, and Adjunct Professor of Mathematics," in a little collegiate institute with
big pretensions in one of the suburbs of Philadelphia.
In short, he had been knocked about in the world until
he had acquired considerable confidence in his ability to
earn a living at almost anything he might undertake.

Under the circumstances, therefore, it is not probable
that this energetic and self-confident young gentleman
would have suffered the loss of his professorship to annoy
him very seriously if it had not been accompanied by the
other trouble mentioned.    Indeed, the two had come so
closely together, and were so intimately connected in
other ways, that Mr. Robert Pagebrook was inclined to
wonder, as he lay there in bed, whether there might not
exist between them somewhere the relation of cause and
effect.    Whether there really was any other than an

accidental blending of the two events I am sure I do not know ; and the reader is at liberty, after hearing the brief story of their happening, to take either side he prefers of the question raised in Mr. Rob's mind. For myself, I find it impossible to determine the point. But here is the story, as young Pagebrook turned it over and over in his mind in spite of himself.

President Currier, of the collegiate institute, had a daughter, Miss Nellie, who wanted to study Latin more than anything else in the world. President Currier particularly disliked conjugations and parsings and everything else pertaining to the study of language ; and so it happened that as Miss Nellie was quite a good-looking and agreeable damsel, our young friend Pagebrook volunteered to give her the coveted instruction in her favorite study in the shape of afternoon lessons. The tutor soon discovered that his pupil's earnest wish to learn Latin had been based—as such desires frequently are in the case of young women—upon an entire misapprehension of the nature and difficulty of the study. In fact, Miss Nellie's clearest idea upon the subject of Latin before beginning it was that "it must be *so* nice !" Her progress, therefore, after the first week or two, was certainly not remarkable for its rapidity ; but the tutor persisted. After awhile the young lady said "Latin wasn't nice at all," a remark which she made haste to qualify by assuring her teacher that "it's nice to take lessons in it, though." Finally Miss Nellie ceased to make any pretense of learning the lessons, but somehow the afternoon *séances* over the grammar were continued, though it must be confessed that the talk was not largely of verbs.

By the time commencement day came the occasional presence of Miss Nellie had become a sort of necessity in the young professor's daily existence, and the desire to be with her led him to spend the summer at Cape May, whither her father annually took her for the season. Now Cape May is an expensive place, as watering places usually are, and so Mr. Robert Pagebrook's stay of a little over two months there made a serious reduction in his reserve fund, which was at best a very limited one. Before going to Cape May he had concluded that he was in love with Miss Nellie, and had informed her of the fact. She had expressed, by manner rather than by spoken word, a reasonable degree of pleasure in the knowledge of this fact; but when pressed for a reply to the young gentleman's impetuous questionings, she had prettily avoided committing herself beyond recall. She told him she might possibly come to love him a little after awhile, in a pretty little maidenly way, which satisfied him that she loved him a good deal already. She said she "didn't know" with a tone and manner which convinced him that she did know; and so the Cape May season passed off very pleasantly, with just enough of uncertainty about the position of affairs to keep up an interest in them.

As the season drew near its close, however, Miss Nellie suddenly informed her lover one evening that her dear father had "plans" for her, and that of course they had both been amusing themselves merely; and she said this in so innocent and so sincere a way that for the moment

her stunned admirer believed it as he retired to his room
with an unusual ache in his heart. When the young man
sat down alone, however, and began meditating upon the
events of the past summer, he was unreasonable enough
to accuse the innocent little maiden of very naughty
trifling, and even to think her wanting in honesty and
sincerity. As he sat there brooding over the matter, and
half hoping that Miss Nellie was only trying him for the
purpose of testing the depth of his affection, a servant
brought him a note, which he opened and read. It was a
very formal affair, as the reader will see upon running his
eye over the following copy :

"CAPE MAY, Sept. 10th, 18—.

*Dear Sir:*—It becomes my duty to inform you that
the authorities controlling the collegiate institute's affairs,
having found it necessary to retrench its expenses somewhat, have determined to dispense altogether with the
adjunct professorship of Mathematics, and to distribute
the duties appertaining to the chair of English Language
and Literature among the other members of the faculty.
In consequence of these changes we shall hereafter be de-
prived of your valuable assistance in the collegiate institute. There is yet due you three hundred dollars ($300)
upon your salary for the late collegiate year, and I greatly regret that the treasurer informs me of a present lack
of funds with which to discharge this obligation. I personally promise you, however, that the amount shall be
remitted to whatever address you may give me, on or before the fifteenth day of November next. I send this by

a messenger just as I am upon the point of leaving Cape
May for a brief trip to other parts of the country.   I remain, sir, with the utmost respect,

Your obedient servant,

DAVID CURRIER,

President, etc.

*To Professor Robert Pagebrook."*

This letter had come to Mr. Robert very unexpectedly,
and its immediate consequence had been to send him
hastily back to his city lodgings.   He had arrived late at
night, and finding no matches in his room, which was
situated in a business building where his neighbors were
unknown to him, he had been compelled to go to bed in
the dark, without the possibility of ascertaining whether
or not there were any letters awaiting him on his table.

Our young gentleman was not, ordinarily, of an irri-
table disposition, and trifling things rarely ever disturbed
his equanimity, but he was forced to admit, as he lay
there in bed, that he had been a very unreasonable young
gentleman on several recent occasions, and naturally
enough he began to catalogue his sins of this sort.
Among other things he remembered that he had worked
himself into a temper over the emptiness of the match-
safe ; and this reminded him that he had not even yet
looked to see if there were any letters on the table at his
elbow, much as he had the night previously bewailed the
impossibility of doing so at once.   Somehow this matter
of his correspondence did not seem half so imperative in
its demands upon his attention now that he could read

his letters at once as it had seemed the night before when he could not read them at all. He stretched out his hand rather languidly, therefore, and taking up the half dozen letters which lay on the table, began to turn them over, examining the superscriptions with small show of interest. Breaking one open he muttered, "There's another forty dollars' worth of folly. I did not need that coat, but ordered it expressly for Cape May. The bill must be paid, of course, and here I am, out of work, with no prospects, and about five hundred dollars less money in bank than I ought to have. !"

I am really afraid he closed that sentence with an ejaculation. I have set down an exclamation point to cover the possibility of such a thing.

He went on with his letters. Presently he opened the last but one, and immediately proceeded to open his eyes rather wider than usual. Jumping out of bed he thrust his head out of the door and called

"Moses !"

"*Moses ! !*"

"MOSES ! ! !"

"MOSES ! ! ! !"

# CHAPTER II.

*Mr. Pagebrook is invited to Breakfast.*

AFTER he had waked up whatever echoes there were in the building by his crescendo calling for Moses, besides spoiling the temper of the night editor who was just then in the midst of his first slumber in the room opposite, Mr. Rob remembered that the old colored janitor, who owned the biblical name, and who for a trifling consideration ministered in the capacity of servant to the personal comfort of the occupants of the rooms under his charge, was never known to answer a call. He was sure to be within hearing, but would maintain a profound silence until he had disposed of whatever matter he might happen to have in hand at the moment, after which he would come to the caller in the sedate and dignified way proper to a person of his importance. Remembering this, and hearing some ominous mutterings from the night editor's room, our young gentleman withdrew his head from the corridor, put on his dressing-gown and slippers, and sat down to await the leisurely coming of the serving man.

Taking up the note again he reread it, although he

knew perfectly well everything in it, and began speculating upon what it could possibly mean, knowing all the while that no amount of speculation could throw the slightest ray of light on the subject in the absence of further information. He read it aloud, just as you or I would have done, when there was nobody by to listen. It was as brief as a telegram, and merely said : " Will you please inform me at once whether we may count upon your acceptance of the position offered you ?" It was signed with an unfamiliar name, to which was appended the abbreviated word " Pres't."

" I shall certainly be very happy to inform the gentleman," thought the perplexed young man, "whether he may or may not (by the way he very improperly omits the alternative ' or not' after his ' whether'), whether he may or may not 'count upon' (I must look up that expression and see if there is good authority for its use), whether he may or may not count upon my acceptance of the position offered me, just as soon as I can inform myself upon the matter. As I have not at present the slightest idea of what the 'position' is, it is somewhat difficult for me to make up my mind concerning it. However, as I am without employment and uncomfortably short of money, there seems to be every probability that my unknown correspondent's proposition, whatever it is, will be favorably considered. Moses will come after awhile, I suppose, and he probably has the other letter caged as a 'vallable.' Let me see what we have here from William."

With this our young gentleman opened his only re-

maining letter, which he had already discovered by a
glance at the postmark was from a Virginian cousin.    It
was a mere note, in which his cousin wrote :

"A little matter of business takes me to Philadelphia
next week.   Shall be at Girard Ho., Thrs^d morn'g.
Meet me there at breakfast, but don't come too early.
Train won't get in till three, so I'll sleep a little late.
Sh'd you wake me too early, I'll be as cross as a $20 bank-
note, and make a bad impression on you."

An amused smile played over Mr. Robert's face as he
read this note over and over.   What he was thinking I
do not know.   Aloud he said :

"What a passion my cousin has for abbreviations !
One would think he had a grudge against words from the
way in which he cuts them up.   And what a figure of
speech that is !   'As cross as a twenty-dollar bank-note !'
Let me see.   I may safely assume that the letters 'T h r s'
with an elevated 'd' mean Thursday, and as this is
Thursday, and as the letter was written last week, and as
my watch tells me it is now ten o'clock, and as my boots
are still unblacked, and as Moses has not yet made his
appearance, it seems altogether probable that my cousin's
breakfast will be postponed until the middle of the day
if he waits for me to help him eat it.   I am afraid he
will be as cross as half a dozen bank notes of the largest
denomination issued when we meet."

"Did you call, sah ?" asked Moses, coming very deliberately into the room.

"I am under the impression that I did, though it requires an extraordinary exercise of the memory to recall

an event which happened so long ago. Have you any 'vallables' for me?"

Moses *thought* he had. This was as near an approach to anything like a positive statement as Moses ever made. He would go to his room and ascertain. Among many other evidences of unusual wisdom on the part of the old negro was this, that he believed himself fully capable of recognizing a valuable letter whenever he saw it; and it was one of his self-imposed duties, whenever the post brought letters for any absent member of his constituency, to look them over and sequestrate all the "vallables" until the return of the owner, so that they might be delivered with his own hand. Returning now he brought two "vallables" for Mr. Pagebrook. One of them was a printed circular, but the other proved to be the desired letter, which was a formal tender of a professorship in a New England college, with an entirely satisfactory salary attached. Accompanying the official notice of election was a note informing him that his duties, in the event of acceptance, would not begin until the first of January, the engagement of the retiring professor terminating at that time.

Under the influence of this news our young friend's face brightened quite as perceptibly as his boots did in the hands of the old servitor. He wrote his letter of acceptance at once, and then proceeded to dress for breakfast at the Girard House, whither he walked with as light a step and as cheerful a bearing as if he had not been a sadly disappointed lover at all.

# CHAPTER III.

### *Mr. Pagebrook Eats his Breakfast.*

ROBERT PAGEBROOK had never seen his cousin, and yet they were not altogether strangers to each other. Robert's father and William Barksdale's mother were brother and sister, and Shirley, the old Virginian homestead, which had been in the family for nearly two centuries, had passed to young Barksdale's mother by the voluntary act of Robert's father when, upon coming of age, he had gone west to try his fortune in a busier world than that of the Old Dominion. The two boys, William and Robert, had corresponded quite regularly in boyhood and quite irregularly after they grew up, and so they knew each other pretty well, though, as I have said, they had never met.

"I am glad, very glad to see you, William," said Robert as he grasped his cousin's hand.

"Now don't, I beg of you. Call me Billy, or Will, or anything else you choose, old fellow, but don't call me William, whatever you do. Nobody ever did but father, and he never did except of mornings when I wouldn't get up. Then he'd sing out 'Will-*yum*' with a sort of a horsewhip snap at the end of it. 'William' always reminds me of disturbed slumbers. Call me Billy, and I'll call you Bob. I'll do that anyhow, so you might as well fall into familiar ways. But come, tell me how you are and all about yourself. You haven't written to me since the flood; forgot to receive my last letter I suppose."

"Probably I did. I have been forgetting a good many things. But I hope I have not kept you too long from your breakfast, and especially that I have not made you 'as cross as a twenty dollar bank-note.' Pray tell me what you meant by that figure of speech, will you not? I am curious to know where you got it and why."

"Ha! ha!" laughed Billy. "You'll have a lively time of it if you mean to unravel all my metaphors. Let me see. I must have referred to the big X's they print on the bank bills, or something of that sort. But let's go to breakfast at once. I'm as hungry as a village editor. We can talk over a beefsteak, or you can at least. I mean to be as still as a mill-pond of a cloudy night while you tell me all about yourself."

And over their breakfast they talked. But in telling his story, while he remembered to mention all the details of his situation losing and his situation getting, Mr. Robert somehow forgot to say anything about his other disappointment. He soon learned to know and to like his cousin, and, which was more to the purpose, he began to enjoy him right heartily, in his own way, bantering him on his queer uses of English, half in sport, half in earnest, until the Virginian declared that they had grown as familiar with each other "as a pair of Irishmen at a wake."

"I suppose you're off at once for your new place, a'n't you? This is September," said Billy after his cousin had finished so much of his story as he cared to reveal.

"No," said Robert. "My duties will not begin until January, and meantime I must go off on a tramp somewhere to get my muscles, physical and financial, up again. To tell the truth I have been dawdling at Cape May this summer instead of going off to the mountains or the prairies, as I usually do, for a healthful and economical foot journey, and the result is that my legs and arms are sadly run down. I have been spending too much money too, and so cannot afford to stay around Philadelphia until January. I think I must go off to some of the mountain counties, where the people think five dollars a fortune and call anything less than a precipice rising ground."

"Well, I reckon you won't," said the Virginian; "I've been inviting you to the 'home of your fathers' ever since I was born, and this is the very first time I ever got you to own up to a scrap of leisure as big as your thumb nail. I've got you now with nothing to do and nowhere to go, and I mean to take you with me this very evening to Virginia. We'll leave on the eleven o'clock train to-night, get to Richmond to-morrow at two, and go up home next morning in time for snack."

"But, my dear Billy——"

"But, my dear Bob, I won't hear a word, and I won't take no for an answer. That's poz roz and the king's

English. I'm managing this little job. You can give up your rooms to-day, sell out your plunder, and stop expenses. Then you needn't open your pocket-book again for so long that you'll forget how it looks inside. Put a few ninepences into your breeches pocket to throw at darkeys when they hold your horse, and the thing's done. And won't we wake up old Shirley? I tell you it's the delightfulest two hundred year old establishment you ever saw or didn't see. As the Irish attorney said of his ancestral home : ' there isn't a table in the house that hasn't had jigs danced upon it, and there's not a chair that you can't throw at a friend's head without the slightest fear of breaking it.' When we get there we'll have as much fun as a pack of hounds on a fresh trail."

"Upon my word, Billy," said the professor cousin, "your metaphors have the merits of freshness and originality, at the least, though now and then, as in the present instance, they are certainly not very complimentary. However, it just occurs to me that I have been wanting to go to Shirley ' ever since I was born,' if you will allow me to borrow one of your forcible phrases, and this really does seem to be a peculiarly good opportunity to do so. I am a good deal interested in dialects and provincialisms, so it would be worth my while to visit you, if for no other reason, because my stay at Shirley will give me an excellent opportunity to study some of your own expressions. ' Poz roz,' now, is entirely new to me, and I might make something out of it in a philological way."

"Upon my word " said Mr. Billy, "that's a polite

speech. If you'll only say you'll go, though, I don't care the value of a herring's left fore foot what use you make of me. I'm yours to command and ready for any sport that suits you, unless you take a notion to throw rocks at me."

"Pray tell me, Billy, do Virginians ever throw rocks? I am interested in muscle, and should greatly like to see some one able to throw rocks. I have paid half a dollar many a time to see a man lift extraordinary weights, but the best of the showmen never dream of handling anything heavier than cannon-balls. It would be decidedly entertaining to see a man throwing rocks and things of that sort about, even if he were to use both hands in doing it."

"Nonsense," said Billy; "I'm not one of your students getting a dictionary lesson. Waiter!"

"What will you have, sir?" asked the waiter.

"Some hot biscuit, please."

"They a'n't no hot biscuits, sir."

"Well some hot rolls then, or hot bread of some sort. Cold bread for breakfast is an abomination."

"They a'n't no hot bread in the house, sir. We never keep none. Hot bread a'n't healthy, sir."

"You impertinent——"

"My dear Billy," said Mr. Bob, "pray keep your temper. 'Impertinent' is not the word you wish to use. The *man* can not well be impertinent. He is a trifle impudent, I admit, but we can afford to overlook the impudence of his remark for the sake of the philological interest it has. Waiter, you ought to know, inasmuch as you have been brought up in a land of free schools, that two negatives, in English, destroy each other, and are equivalent to an affirmative; but the matter in which I am most interested just now is your remark that hot bread is not *healthy.* Your statement is perfectly true, and it would have been equally true if you had omitted the qualifying adjective 'hot.' No bread can be 'healthy,' because health and disease are not attributes or conditions of inanimate things. You probably meant, however, that hot bread is not wholesome, a point on which my friend here, who eats hot bread every day of his life, would naturally take issue with you. Please bring us some buttered toast."

The waiter went away bewildered—questioning the sanity of Mr. Bob in all probability; a questioning in which Billy was half inclined to join him.

"What on earth do you mean, Bob, by talking in that way to a waiter who don't know the meaning of one word in five that you use?"

"Well, I meant for one thing to keep you from losing your temper and so spoiling your digestion. Human motives are complicated affairs, and hence I am by no means sure that I can further unravel my purpose in this case."

"Return we to our muttons, then," said Billy; "I'll finish the business that brought me here, which is only to be present at the taking of a short deposition, by two or three o'clock. While I'm at it you can get your traps together, send your trunk to the depot, and get back here to dinner by four. Then we must get through the rest of the time the best way we can, and at eleven we'll be off. I'm crazy to see you with Phil once."

"Phil, who is he?"

"Oh! Phil is a character—a colored one. I want to see how his 'dialect' will affect you. I'm half afraid you'll go crazy, though, under it."

"Tell me—"

"No, I won't describe Phil, because I can't, and no more can anybody else. Phil must be seen to be appreciated. But come, I'm off for the notary's, and you must get you gone too, for you mustn't be late at dinner —that's poz."

With this the two young men separated, the Virginian lawyer to attend to the taking of some depositions, and his cousin to surrender his lodgings, pack his trunk, and make such other arrangements as were necessary for his journey.

This opportunity to visit the old homestead where his father had passed his boyhood was peculiarly welcome to Mr. Robert just now. There had always been to him a sort of glamour about the names Virginia and Shirley. His father's stories about his own childhood had made a deep impression on the mind of the boy, and to him Shirley was a palace and Virginia a fairy land. Whenever, in childhood, he was allowed to call a calf or a pig his own, he straightway bestowed upon it one or the other of the charmed names, and fancied that the animal grew stronger and more beautiful as a consequence. He had always intended to go to Shirley, but had never done so; just as you and I, reader, have always meant to do

several scores of things that we have never done, though
we can hardly say why. Just now, however, Mr. Billy's
plan for his cousin was more than ever agreeable to Mr.
Robert for various present and unusual reasons. He
knew next to nobody in or about Philadelphia outside the
precincts of the collegiate institute, and to hunt up
acquaintances inside that institution was naturally
enough not exactly to his taste. He had several months
of time to dispose of in some way, and until Billy suggested the visit to Virginia, the best he had been able to
do in the way of devising a time-killer was to plan a soli-
tary wandering among the mountainous districts of
Pennsylvania. Ordinarily he would have enjoyed such a
journey very much, but just now he knew that Mr.
Robert Pagebrook could hardly find a less agreeable
companion than Mr. Robert Pagebrook himself. That
little affair with Miss Nellie Currier kept coming up in
his memory, and if the reader be a man it is altogether
probable that he knows precisely how the memory of that
story affected our young gentleman. He wanted company, and he wanted change, and he wanted out-door
exercise, and where could he find all these quite so abun-
dant as at an old Virginian country house ? His love for
Miss Nellie, he was sure, was a very genuine one ; but he
was equally sure that it was hopeless. Indeed, now that
he knew the selfish insincerity of the damsel he did not
even wish that his suit had prospered. This, at any rate,
is what he thought, as you did, my dear sir, when you
first learned what the word "Another" means when
printed with a big A ; and, thinking this, he felt that

the first thing to be done in the matter was to forget Miss Nellie and his love for her as speedily as possible. How far he succeeded in doing this we shall probably see in the sequel. At present we have to do with the attempt only. New scenes and new people, Mr. Pagebrook thought, would greatly aid him in his purpose, and so the trip to Virginia seemed peculiarly fitting. It thus comes about that the scene of this young man's story suddenly shifts from Philadelphia to a Virginian country house, in spite of all I can do to preserve the dramatic unity of place. Ah! if I were *making* this story now, I could confine it to a single room, compress its action into a single day, and do other dramatic and highly proper things; but as Mr. Robert Pagebrook and his friends were not stage people, and, moreover, as they were not aware that their goings and comings would ever weave themselves into the woof of a story at all, they utterly failed to regulate their actions in accordance with critical rules, and went roving about over the country quite in a natural way and without the slightest regard for my convenience.

# CHAPTER IV.

*Mr. Pagebrook learns something about the Customs of the Country.*

WHEN our two young men reached the station at which they were to leave the cars, they found awaiting them there the lumbering old carriage which had been a part of the Shirley establishment ever since Mr. Billy could remember. This vehicle was known to everybody in the neighborhood as the Shirley carriage, not because it was older or clumsier or uglier than its fellows, for indeed it was not, but merely because every carriage in a Virginian neighborhood is known to everybody quite as well as its owner is. To Mr. Robert Pagebrook, however, the vehicle presented itself as an antique and a curiosity. Its body was suspended by leathern straps which came out of some high semicircular springs at the back, and it was thus raised so far above the axles that one could enter it only by mounting quite a stairway of steps, which unfolded themselves from its interior. Swinging thus by its leathern straps, the great heavy carriage body really seemed to have no support at all, and Mr. Robert found it necessary to exercise all the faith there was in him in order to believe that to get inside of the vehicle was not a sure and speedy way of securing two or three broken bones. He got in, however, at his cousin's invitation, and soon discovered that although the motion of the suspended carriage body closely resembled that of a fore and aft schooner in a gale, it was by no means unpleasant, as the worst that the roughest road could do was to make the vibratory motion a trifle more decided than usual in its nature. A jolt was simply impossible.

As soon as he got his sea legs on sufficiently to keep himself tolerably steady on his seat, Mr. Rob began to look at the country or, more properly, to study the roadside, there being little else visible, so thickly grew the trees and underbrush on each side.

"How far must we drive before reaching Shirley?" he asked after awhile, as the carriage stopped for the opening of a gate.

"About four miles now," said his cousin. "It's five miles, or nearly that, from the Court House."

"The court house? Where is that?"

"O the village where we left the train! That's the Court House."

"Ah! you Virginians call a village a court house, do you?"

"Certainly, when it's the county-seat and a'n't much else. Now and then court houses put on airs and call themselves names, but they don't often make much of it. There's Powhatan Court House now, I believe it tried to get itself called 'Scottsville,' or something of that sort, but nobody knows it as anything but Powhatan Court

House. Our county-seat has always been modest, and if it has any name I never heard of it."

"That's one interesting custom of the country, at any rate. Pray tell me, is it another of your customs to dispense wholly with public roads? I ask for information merely, and the question is suggested by the fact that we seem to have driven away from the Court House by the private road which we are still following."

"Why, this isn't a private road. It's one of the principal public roads of the county."

"How about these gates then?" asked Robert as the negro boy who rode behind the carriage jumped down to open another.

"Well, what about them?"

"Why, I never saw a gate across a public thoroughfare before. Do you really permit such things in Virginia?"

"O yes! certainly. It saves a great deal of fencing, and the Court never refuses permission to put up a gate in any reasonable place, only the owner is bound to make it easy to open on horseback—or, as you would put it, 'by a person riding on horseback.' You see I'm growing circumspect in my choice of words since I've been with you. May be you'll reform us all, and make us talk tolerably good English before you go back. If you do, I'll give you some 'testimonials' to your worth as a professor."

"But about those gates, Billy. I am all the more interested in them now that I know them as another 'custom of the country.' How do their owners keep them shut? Don't people leave them open pretty often?"

"Never; a Virginian is always 'on honor' so far as his

neighbors are concerned, and the man who would leave a neighbor's gate open might as well take to stealing at once for all the difference it would make in his social standing."

It was not only the gates, but the general appearance of the road as well, that astonished young Pagebrook : a public road, consisting of a single carriage track, with a grass plat on each side, fringed with thick undergrowth and overhung by the branches of great trees, was to him a novelty, and a very pleasant novelty too, in which he was greatly interested.

"Who lives there?" asked Robert, as a large house came into view.

"That's The Oaks, Cousin Edwin's place."

"And who is your Cousin Edwin?"

"*My* Cousin Edwin? He's yours too, I reckon. Cousin Edwin Pagebrook. He is our second cousin or, as the old ladies put it, first cousin once removed."

"Pray tell me what a first cousin once removed is, will you not, Billy? I am wholly ignorant on the subject of cousinhood in its higher branches, and as I understand that a good deal of stress is laid upon relationships of this sort in Virginia, I should like to inform myself in advance if possible."

"I really don't know whether I can or not. Any of the old ladies will lay it all out to you, illustrating it with their keys arranged like a genealogical tree. I don't know much about it, but I reckon I can make you understand this much, as I have Cousin Edwin's case to go by. It's a 'case in point' as we lawyers say. Let's see.

Cousin Edwin's grandfather was our great grandfather; then his father was our grandfather's brother, and that makes him first cousin to my mother and your father. Now I would call mother's first cousin my second cousin, but the old ladies, who pay a good deal of attention to these matters, say not. They say that my mother's or my father's first cousin is my first cousin once removed, and his children are my second cousins, and they prove it all, too, with their keys."

"Well then," asked Robert, "if that is so, what is the exact relationship between Cousin Edwin's children and my father or your mother?"

"O don't! You bewilder me. I told you I didn't know anything about it. You must get some old lady to explain it with her keys, and when she gets through you won't know who you are, to save you."

"That is encouraging, certainly," said Mr. Robert.

"O it's no matter! You're safe enough in calling everybody around here 'cousin' if you're sure they a'n't any closer kin. The fact is, all the best families here have intermarried so often that the relationships are all mixed up, and we always claim kin when there is any ghost of a chance for it. Besides, the Pagebrooks are the biggest tadpoles in the puddle; and so, if they don't 'cousin' all their kin-folks people think they're stuck-up."

"Thank you, Billy; but tell me, am I, being a Pagebrook, under any consequent obligation to consider myself a tadpole during my stay in Virginia?"

Billy's only answer was a laugh.

"Now, Billy," Robert resumed, "tell me about the

people of Shirley. I am sadly ignorant, you understand, and I do not wish to make mistakes. Begin at
top, and tell me how I shall call them all."

"Well, there's father; you will call him Uncle Carter,
of course. He is Col. Carter Barksdale, you know."

"I knew his name was Carter, of course, but I did not
know he had ever been a military man."

"A military man! No, he never was. What made
you think that?"

"Why you called him 'Colonel.'"

"O that's nothing! You'll find every gentleman past
middle age wearing some sort of title or other. They
call father 'Colonel Barksdale,' and Cousin Edwin 'Major
Pagebrook,' though neither of them ever saw a tent
that I know of."

"Ah! another interesting custom of the country.
But pray go on."

"Well, mother is 'Aunt Mary,' you know, and then
there's Aunt Catherine."

"Indeed! who is she? Is she my aunt?"

"I really don't know. Let me see. No, I reckon not;
nor mine either, for that matter. I think she's father's
fourth or fifth cousin, with a remove or two added,
possibly, but you must call her 'Aunt' anyhow; we all
do, and she'd never forgive you if you didn't. You see
she knew your father, and I reckon he called her 'Aunt.'
It's a way we have here. She is a maiden lady, you
understand, and Shirley is her home. You'll find somebody of that sort in nearly every house, and they're a
delightful sort of somebody, too, to have round. She'll

post you up on relationships. She can use up a whole
key-basket full of keys, and run 'em over by name back-
wards or forwards, just as you please. You needn't follow her though if you object to a headache. All 'you've
got to do is to let her tell you about it, and you say 'yes'
now and then. She puts me through every week or so.
Then there's Cousin Sudie, my father's niece and ward.
She's been an orphan almost all her life, and so she's
always lived with us. Father is her guardian, and he
always calls her 'daughter.' You'll call her 'Cousin
Sue,' of course."

"Then she is akin to me too, is she?"

"Of course. She's father's own brother's child."

"But, Billy, your father is only my uncle by marriage,
and I do not understand how——"

"O bother! If you're going to count it up, I reckon
there a'n't any real relationship; but she's your cousin,
anyhow, and you'll offend her if you refuse to own it.
Call her 'Cousin,' and be done with it."

"Being one of the large Pagebrook tadpoles, I suppose
I must. However, in the case of a young lady, I shall
not find it difficult, I dare say."

# CHAPTER V.

## *Mr. Pagebrook makes Some Acquaintances.*

MR. ROBERT had often heard of "an Old Virginian welcome," but precisely what constituted it
he never knew until the carriage in which he rode drove
around the "circle" and stopped in front of the Shirley
mansion.    The first thing which struck him as peculiar
about the preparations made for his reception was the
large number of small negroes who thought their presence
necessary to the occasion.    Little black faces grinned at
him from behind every tree, and about a dozen of them
peered out from a safe position behind "ole mas'r and ole
missus."    Mr. Billy had telegraphed from Richmond
announcing the coming of his guest, and so every darkey
on the plantation knew that "Mas' Joe's son" was "a
comin' wid Mas' Billy from de Norf," and every one that
could find a safe hiding place in the yard was there to
see him come.

Col. Barksdale met him at the carriage while the
ladies were in waiting on the porch, as anybody but a Virginian would put it—*in* the porch, as they themselves
would have phrased it.    The welcome was of the right
hearty order which nobody ever saw outside of Virginia—

a welcome which made the guest feel himself at once a very part of the establishment.

Inside the house our young friend found himself sorely puzzled.   The furniture was old in style but very elegant, a thing for which he was fully prepared, but it stood upon absolutely bare white floors.   There were both damask and lace curtains at the windows, but not a vestige of carpet was anywhere to be seen.   Mr. Robert said nothing, but wondered silently whether it was possible that he had arrived in the midst of house-cleaning. Conversation, luncheon, and finally dinner at four, occupied his attention, however, and after dinner the whole family gathered in the porch—for really I believe the Virginians are right about that preposition.   I will ask Mr. Robert himself some day.

He soon found himself thoroughly at home in the old family mansion, among relatives who had never been strangers to him in any proper sense of the term.   Not only was Mrs. Barksdale his father's sister, but Col. Barksdale himself had been that father's nearest friend. The two had gone west together to seek their fortunes there ; but the Colonel had returned after a few years to practice his profession in his native state and ultimately to marry his friend's sister.   Mr. Robert soon felt himself literally at home, therefore, and the feeling was intensely enjoyable, too, to a young man who for ten years had not known any home other than that of a bachelor's quarters in a college community.   His reception at Shirley had not been the greeting of a guest but rather the welcoming of a long wandering son of the house.

To his relatives there he seemed precisely that, and their feeling in the case soon became his own. This "clannishness," as it is called, may not be peculiar to Virginia of all the states, but I have never seen it half so strongly manifested anywhere else as there.

Toward evening Maj. Pagebrook and his son Ewing rode over to call upon their cousin Robert, and after the introductions were over, "Cousin Edwin" went on to talk of Robert's father, for whom he had felt an unusual degree of affection, as all the relatives had, for that matter, Robert's father having been an especial favorite in the family. Then the conversation became more general.

"When are you going to cut that field of tobacco by the prize barn, Cousin Edwin?" asked Billy. "I see it's ripening pretty rapidly."

"Yes, it is getting pretty ripe in spots, and I wanted to put the hands into it yesterday," replied Maj. Pagebrook; "but Sarah Ann thought we'd better keep them plowing for wheat a day or two longer, and now I'm afraid it's going to rain before I can get a first cutting done."

"How much did you get for the tobacco you sent to Richmond the other day, Edwin?" asked the colonel.

"Only five dollars and three cents a hundred, average."

"You'd have done a good deal better if you'd sold in the spring, wouldn't you?"

"Yes, a good deal. I wanted to sell then, but Sarah Ann insisted on holding it till fall. By the way, I'm going to put all my lots, except the one by the creek, in corn next year, and raise hardly any tobacco."

"All but the creek lot? Why that's the only good corn land you have, Edwin, and it isn't safe to put tobacco in it either, for it overflows a little."

"Yes, I know it. But Sarah Ann is discouraged by the price we got for tobacco this year, and doesn't want me to plant the lots next season at all."

"Why didn't you bring Cousin Sarah Ann over and come to dinner to-day, Cousin Edwin?" asked Miss Barksdale, coming out of the dining-room, key-basket in hand, to speak to the guests.

"Oh! we've only one carriage horse now, you know. I sold the black last week, and haven't been able to find another yet."

"Sold the black! Why, what was that for, Cousin Ed! I thought you specially liked him?" said Billy.

"So I did; but Sarah Ann didn't like a black and a gray together, and she wouldn't let me sell the gray on any terms, though I could have matched the black at once. Winger has a colt well broken that's a perfect match for him. Come, Ewing, we must be going. Sarah Ann said we must be home to tea without fail. You'll come to The Oaks, Robert, of course. Sarah Ann will expect you very soon, and you mustn't stand on ceremony, you know, but come as often as you can while you stay at Shirley."

"What do you think of Cousin Edwin, Bob?" asked Billy when the guests had gone.

"That he is a very excellent person, and——"

"And what? Speak out. Let's hear what you think."

"Well, that he is a very dutiful husband."

"Bob, I'd give a pretty for your knack at saying things. Your tongue's as soft as a feather bed. But wait till you know the madam. You'll say——."

"My son, you shouldn't prejudice Robert against people he doesn't know. Sarah Ann has many good qualities—I suppose."

"Well, then, I don't suppose anything of the sort, else she would have found out how good a man Cousin Edwin is long ago, and would have behaved herself better every way."

"William, you are uncharitable!"

"Not a bit of it, mother. Your charity is like a microscope when it is hunting for something good to say of people. Did you ever hear of the dead Dutchman?"

"Do pray, Billy, don't tell me any of your anecdotes now."

"Just this one, mother. There was a dead Dutchman who had been the worst Dutchman in the business. When the people came to sit up with his corpse—don't run, mother, I'm nearly through—they couldn't find anything good to say about him, and as they didn't want to say anything bad there was a profound silence in the room. Finally one old Dutchman, heaving a sigh, remarked : 'Vell, Hans vas vone goot schmoker, anyhow.' Let me see. Cousin Sarah Ann gives good dinners, anyhow, only she piles too much on the table. See how charitable I am, mother. I have actually found and designated the madam's one good point."

"Come, come, my son," said the colonel, "you shouldn't talk so."

Shortly after tea the two young men pleaded the weariness of travelers in excuse for an early bed going. Mr. Bob was offered his choice between occupying alone the Blue Room, which is the state guest chamber in most Virginian houses, and taking a bed in Billy's room. He promptly chose the latter, and when they were alone, he turned to his cousin and asked :

"Billy, have you such a thing as a dictionary about ?"

"Nothing but a law dictionary, I believe. Will that do ?"

"Really I do not know. Perhaps it might."

"What do you want to find ?" asked Billy.

"I only wish to ascertain whether or not we arrived here in time for 'snack.' You said we would, I believe."

"Well, we did, didn't we ?"

"That is precisely what I wish to find out. Having never heard of 'snack' until you mentioned it as one of the things we should find at Shirley, I have been curious to know what it is like, and so I have been watching for it ever since we got here. Pray tell me what it is ?"

"Well, that's a good one. I must tell Sudie that, and get her to introduce you formally to-morrow."

"It is another interesting custom of the country, I suppose."

"Indeed it is ; and it isn't one of those customs that are 'more honored in the breach than the observance,' either."

# CHAPTER VI.

### *Mr. Pagebrook makes a Good Impression.*

YOUNG Pagebrook was an early riser. Not that he was afflicted with one of those unfortunate consciences which make of early rising a penance, by any means. He was not prejudiced against lying abed, nor bigoted about getting up. He quoted no adages on the subject, and was not illogical enough to believe that getting up early and yawning for an hour or two every morning would bring health, wisdom, or wealth to anybody. In short, he was an early riser not on principle but of necessity. Somehow his eyelids had a way of popping themselves open about sunrise or earlier, and his great brawny limbs could not be kept in bed long after this happened. He got up for precisely the same reason that most people lie abed, namely, because there was nothing else to do. On the morning after his arrival at Shirley he awoke early and heard two things which attracted his attention. The first was a sound which puzzled him more than a little. It was a steady, monotonous scraping of a most unaccountable kind—somewhat like the sound of a carpenter's plane and somewhat like that of a saw. Had it been out of doors he would have thought nothing of it; but clearly it was in the house, and not only so, but in every part of the house except the bedrooms. Scrape, scrape, scrape, scrape, scrape. What it meant he could not guess. As he lay there wondering about it he heard another sound, greatly more musical, at which he jumped out of bed and began dressing, wondering at this sound, too, quite as much as at the other, though he knew perfectly well that this was nothing more than a human voice—Miss Sudie's, to wit. He wondered if there ever was such a voice before or ever would be again. Not that the young woman was singing, for she was doing nothing of the sort. She was merely giving some directions to the servants about household matters, but her voice was music nevertheless, and Mr. Bob made up his mind to hear it to better advantage by going down-stairs at once. Now I happen to know that this young woman's voice was in no way peculiar to herself. Every well-bred girl in Virginia has the same rich, full, soft tone, and they all say, as she did, "grauss," "glauss" "bausket," "cyarpet," "cyart," "gyarden," and "gyirl." But it so happened that Mr. Bob had never heard a Virginian girl talk before he met Miss Barksdale, and to him her rich German a's and the musical tones of her voice were peculiarly her own. Perhaps all these things would have impressed him differently if "Cousin Sudie" had been an ugly girl. I have no means of determining the point, inasmuch as "Cousin Sudie" was certainly anything else than ugly.

Mr. Robert made a hasty toilet and descended to the

great hall, or passage, as they call it in Virginia. As he did so he discovered the origin of the scraping sound which had puzzled him, as it puzzles everybody else who hears it for the first time. Dry "pine tags" (which is Virginian for the needles of the pine) were scattered all over the floors, and several negro women were busy polishing the hard white planks by rubbing them with an indescribable implement made of a section of log, a dozen corn husks ("shucks," the Virginians call them—a "corn husk" in Virginia signifying a *cob* always), and a pole for handle.

"Good morning, Cousin Robert. You're up soon," said the little woman, coming out of the dining-room and putting a soft, warm little hand in his great palm.

Now to young Pagebrook this was a totally new use of the word "soon," and I dare say he would have been greatly interested in it but for the fact that the trim little woman who stood there, key-basket in hand, interested him more.

"You've caught me in the midst of my housekeeping, but never mind; only be careful, or you'll slip on the pine tags; they're as slippery as glass."

"And is that the reason they are scattered on the floor?"

"Yes, we polish with them. Up North you wax your floors instead, don't you?"

"Yes, for balls and the like, I believe, but commonly we have carpets."

"What! in summer time, too?"

"O yes! certainly. Why not?"

"Why, they're so warm. We take ours up soon in the spring, and never put them down again until fall."

This time Mr. Robert observed the queer use of the word "soon," but said nothing about it. He said instead:

"What a lovely morning it is! How I should like to ride horseback in this air!"

"Would you let me ride with you?" asked the little maiden.

"Such a question, Cousin Sudie!"

Now I am free to confess that this last remark was unworthy Mr. Pagebrook. If not ungrammatical, it is at least of questionable construction, and so not at all like Mr. Pagebrook's usage. But the demoralizing effect of Miss Sudie Barksdale's society did not stop here by any means, as we shall see in due time.

"If you'd really like to ride, I'll have the horses brought," said the little lady.

"And you with me?"

"Yes, if I may."

"I shall be more than happy."

"Dick, run up to the barn and tell Uncle Polidore to saddle Patty for me and Graybeard for your Mas' Robert. Do you hear? Excuse me, Cousin Robert, and I'll put on my habit."

Ten minutes later the pair reined in their horses on the top of a little hill, to look at the sunrise. The morning was just cool enough to be thoroughly pleasant, and the exhilaration which comes of nothing else so surely as of rapid riding began to tell upon the spirits of

both.   Cousin Sudie was a good rider and a graceful one,
and she knew it.    Robert's riding hitherto had been
done, for the most part, in cities, and on smooth roads ;
but he held his horse with a firm hand, and controlled
him perforce of a strong will, which, with great personal
fearlessness and a habit of doing well whatever he undertook to do at all, and undertaking whatever was expected of him, abundantly supplied the lack he had of
experience in the rougher riding of Virginia on the less
perfectly trained horses in use there.    He was a stalwart
fellow, with shapely limbs and perfect ease of movement,
so that on horseback he was a very agreeable young
gentleman to look at, a fact of which Miss Sudie speedily
became conscious.    Her rides were chiefly without a
cavalier, as they were usually taken early in the morning
before her cousin Billy thought of getting up ; and
naturally enough she enjoyed the presence of so agreeable
a young gentleman as Mr. Rob certainly was, and her
enjoyment of his company—she being a woman—was not
diminished in the least by the discovery that to his intellectual and social accomplishments, which were very
genuine, there were added a handsome face, a comely
person, and a manly enthusiasm for out-door exercise.
When he pulled some wild flowers which grew by the
road-side without dismounting—a trick he had picked up
somewhere—she wondered at the ease and grace with
which it was done ; when he added to the flowers a little
cluster of purple berries from a wild vine, of which I do
not know the name, and a sprig of sumac, still wet with
dew, she admired his taste ; and when he gallantly asked

leave to twine the whole into her hair, for her hat had come off, as good-looking young women's hats always do on such occasions, she thought him "just nice."

It is really astonishing how rapidly acquaintanceships form under favorable circumstances. These two young people were shy, both of them, and on the preceding day had hardly spoken to each other at all. When they mounted their horses that morning they were almost strangers, and they might have remained only half acquaintances for a week or a fortnight but for that morning's ride. They were gone an hour, perhaps, in all, and when they sat down to breakfast they were on terms of easy familiarity and genuine friendship.

## CHAPTER VII.

### *Mr. Pagebrook Learns Several Things.*

AFTER breakfast Robert walked out with Billy to see the negroes at work cutting tobacco, an interesting operation always, and especially so when one sees it for the first time.

"Gilbert," said Billy to his "head man," "did you find any ripe enough to cut in the lot there by the prize barn ?"

"No sah ; dat's de greenest lot of tobawkah on de plantation, for all 'twas plaunted fust. I dunno what to make uv it."

"Why, Billy, I thought Cousin Edwin owned the ' prize ' barn !" said Robert.

"So he does—his."

"Are there two of them then ?"

"Two of them ? What do you mean ? Every plantation has its prize barn, of course."

"Indeed ! Who gives the prizes ?"

"Ha ! ha ! Bob, that's good ; only you'd better ask *me* always when you want to know about things here, else you'll get yourself laughed at. A prize barn is simply the barn in which we prize tobacco."

" And what is 'prizing' tobacco ?"

" Possibly 'prize' a'n't good English, Bob, but it's the standard Ethiopian for pressing, and everybody here uses it. We press the tobacco in hogsheads, you know, and we call it prizing. It never struck me as a peculiarly Southern use of the word, but perhaps it is for all that. You're as sharp set as a circular saw after dialect, a'n't you ?"

" I really do not know precisely how sharp set a circular saw is, but I am greatly interested in your peculiar uses of English, certainly."

Upon returning to the house Billy said :

" Bob I must let you take care of yourself for two or three hours now, as I have some papers to draw up and they won't wait. Next week is court week, and I've got a great deal to do between now and then. But you're at home you know, old fellow."

So saying Mr. Billy went to his office, which was situated in the yard, while Robert strolled into the house. Looking into the dining-room he saw there Cousin Sudie. Possibly the young gentleman was looking for her. I am sure I do not know. But whether he had expected to find her there or not, he certainly felt some little surprise as he looked at her.

" Why, Cousin Sudie, is it possible that you are washing the dishes ?"

" O certainly ! and the plates and cups too. In fact, I wash up all the things once a day."

" Pray tell me, cousin, precisely what you understand by ' dishes,' if I'm not intruding," said Robert.

"O not at all ! come in and sit down. You'll find it pleasanter there by the window. 'Dishes ?' Why, that is a dish, and that and that," pointing to them.

"I see. The word 'dishes' is not a generic term in Virginia, but applies only to platters and vegetable dishes. What do you call them in the aggregate, Cousin Sudie ? I mean plates, platters, cups, saucers, and everything."

"Why 'things,' I suppose. We speak of 'breakfast things,' 'tea things,' 'dinner things.' But why were you astonished to see me washing them, Cousin Robert ?"

"Perhaps I ought to have known better, but the fact is I had an impression that Southern ladies were wholly exempt from all work except, perhaps, a little embroidery or some such thing."

"O my ! I wish you could see me during circuit court week, when Uncle Carter and Cousin Billy bring the judge and the lawyers home with them at all sorts of odd hours ; and they always bring the hungriest ones there are too. I fall at once into a chronic state of washing up things, and don't recover until court is over."

"But really, cousin—pardon me if I am inquisitive, for I am greatly interested in this life here in Virginia, it is so new to me—how is it that *you* must wash up things at all ?"

"Why, I carry the keys, you know. I'm housekeeper."

"Well, but you have servants enough, certainly, and to spare."

"O yes ! but every lady washes up the things at least once a day. It would never do to trust it altogether to the servants, you know."

"I FALL AT ONCE INTO A CHRONIC STATE OF WASHING UP THINGS."

" None of them are sufficiently careful and trustworthy, do you mean ?"

" Well, not exactly that ; but it's our way here, and if a lady were to neglect it people would think her a poor housekeeper."

" Are there any other duties devolving upon Virginian housekeepers besides ' washing up things ?' You see I am trying to learn all I can of a life which is as charmingly strange to me as that of Turkey or China would be if I were to go to either country."

" Any other duties ? Indeed there are, and you shall learn what they are, if you won't find it stupid to go my rounds with me. I'm going now."

" I should find dullness itself interesting with you as my fellow observer of it."

" Right gallantly said, kind sir," said Miss Sudie, with an exaggerated curtsy. " But if you're going to make pretty speeches I'll get impudent directly. I'm dreadfully given to it anyhow, and I've a notion to say one impudent thing right now."

" Pray do. I pardon you in advance."

" Well, then, what makes you say ' Virginian housekeepers ?' "

" What else should I say ?"

" Why, Virginia housekeepers, of course, like anybody else."

" But ' Virginia ' is not an adjective, cousin. You would not say ' England housekeepers ' or ' France housekeepers,' would you ?" asked Robert.

" No, but I would say ' New York housekeepers,' ' Mas-

sachusetts housekeepers,' or ' New Jersey housekeepers,'
and so I say ' Virginia housekeepers,' too.   I reckon you
would find it a little troublesome to carry out your rule,
wouldn't you, Cousin Robert ?"

"I am fairly beaten, I own ; and in consideration of
my frank acknowledgment of defeat, perhaps you will
permit *me* to be a trifle impudent."

"After that gallant speech you made just now, I can
hardly believe such a thing possible.   But let me hear
you try, please."

"O it's very possible, I assure you !" said Robert.
"See if it is not.   What I want to ask is, why you Virginians so often use the word ' reckon' in the sense of
' think' or ' presume,' as you did a moment since ?"

"Because it's right," said Sudie.

"No, cousin, it is not good English," replied Robert.

"Perhaps not, but it's *good Virginian*, and that's better for my purposes.   Besides, it must be good English.
St. Paul used it twice."

"Did he ?   I was not aware that the Apostle to the
Gentiles spoke English at all."

"Come, Cousin Robert, I must give out dinner now.
Do you want to carry my key-basket ?"

# CHAPTER VIII.

## *Miss Sudie makes an Apt Quotation.*

MY friend who writes novels tells me that there is no other kind of exercise which so perfectly rests an over-tasked brain as riding on horseback does. His theory is that when the mind is overworked it will not quit working at command, but goes on with the labor after the tools have been laid aside. If the worker goes to bed, either he finds it impossible to go to sleep or sleeping he dreams, his mind thus working harder in sleep than if he were awake. Walking, this novelist friend says, affords no relief. On the contrary, one thinks better when walking than at any other time. But on horseback he finds it impossible to confine his thoughts to any subject for two minutes together. He may begin as many trains of thought as he chooses, but he never gets past their beginning. The motion of the animal jolts it all up into a jumble, and rest is the inevitable result. The man's animal spirits rise, in sympathy, perhaps, with those of his horse, and as the animal in him begins to assert itself his intellect yields to its master and suffers itself to become quiescent.

Now it is possible that Mr. Robert Pagebrook had found out this fact about horseback exercise, and determined to profit by it to the extent of securing all the intellectual rest he could during his stay at Shirley. At any rate, his early morning ride with "Cousin Sudie" was repeated, not once, but every day when decided rain did not interfere. He became greatly interested, too, in the Virginian system of housekeeping, and made daily study of it in company with Miss Sudie, whose key-basket he carried as she went her rounds from dining-room to smoke-house, from smoke-house to store-room, from store-room to garden, and from garden to the shady gable of the house, where Miss Sudie "set" the churn every morning, a process which consisted of scalding it out, putting in the cream, and wrapping wet cloths all over the head of it and far up the dasher handle, as a precaution against the possible results of carelessness on the part of the half dozen little darkeys whose daily duty it was to "chun." Mr. Robert soon became well versed in all the mysteries of "giving out" dinner and other things pertaining to the office of housekeeper—an office in which every Virginian woman takes pride, and one in the duties of which every well-bred Virginian girl is thoroughly skilled. (Corollary—good dinners and general comfort.)

Old "Aunty" cooks are always extremely slow of motion, and so the young ladies who carry the keys have a good deal of necessary leisure during their morning rounds. Miss Sudie had a pretty little habit, as a good many other young women there have, of carrying a book in her key-basket, so that she might read while aunt

Kizzey (I really do not know of what proper noun this very common one is an abbreviation) made up her tray. Picking up a volume he found there one morning, Robert continued a desultory conversation by saying :

"You don't read Montaigne, do you, Cousin Sudie ?"

"O yes ! I read everything—or anything, rather. I never saw a book I couldn't get something out of, except Longfellow."

"Except Longfellow !" exclaimed Robert in surprise. "Is it possible you don't enjoy Longfellow ? Why, that is heresy of the rankest kind !"

"I know it is, but I'm a heretic in a good many things. I hate Longfellow's hexameters; I don't like Tennyson ; and I can't understand Browning any better than he understands himself. I know I ought to like them all, as you all up North do, but I don't."

Mr. Robert was shocked. Here was a young girl, fresh and healthy, who could read prosy old Montaigne's chatter with interest ; who knew Pope by heart, and Dryden almost as well ; who read the prose and poetry of the eighteenth century constantly, as he knew ; and who, on a former occasion, had pleaded guilty to a liking for sonnets, but who could find nothing to like in Tennyson, Longfellow, or Browning. Somehow the discovery was not an agreeable one to him though he could hardly say why, and so he chose not to pursue the subject further just then. He said instead :

"That is the queerest Virginianism I've heard yet— 'you all.'"

"It's a very convenient one, you'll admit, and a

Virginian don't care to go far out of his way in such things."

"You will think me critical this morning, Cousin Sudie, but I often wonder at the carelessness, not of Virginians only, but of everybody else, in the use of contractions. 'Don't,' for instance, is well enough as a contraction for 'do not, but nearly everybody uses it, as you did just now, for 'does not.'"

"Do don't lecture me, Cousin Robert. I'm a heretic, I tell you, in grammar."

"'Do don't' is the richest provincialism I have heard yet, Cousin Sudie. I really must make a note of that."

"Cousin Robert, do you read Montaigne ?"

"Sometimes. Why ?"

"Do you remember what he says about custom and grammar ?"

"No. What is it ?"

"He says it, remember, and not I. He says 'they that fight custom with grammar are fools.' What a rude old fellow he was, wasn't he ?"

Mr. Pagebrook suddenly remembered that he was to dine that day at his cousin Edwin's house, and that it was time for him to go, as he intended to walk, Graybeard having fallen lame during that morning's gallop with Miss Sudie.

# CHAPTER IX.

*Mr. Pagebrook Meets an Acquaintance.*

MR. ROBERT left the house on his way to The Oaks in an excellent humor with himself and with everybody else. His cousin Billy and his uncle Col. Barksdale were both absent, in attendance upon a court in another county, and so Mr. Robert had recently been left almost alone with Miss Sudie, and now that they had become the very best of friends our young man enjoyed this state of affairs right heartily. In truth Miss Sudie was a young lady very much to Mr. Robert's taste, in saying which I pay that young gentleman as handsome a compliment as any well regulated man could wish.

Mr. Robert walked briskly out of the front gate and down the road, enjoying the bright sun and the rich coloring of the October woodlands, and making merry in his heart by running over in his memory the chats he had been having of late with the little woman who carried the keys at Shirley. If he had been forced to tell precisely what had been said in those conversations, it must be confessed that a stranger would have found very little of interest in the repetition, but somehow the recollection brought a frequent smile to our young friend's face and put an additional springiness into his step. His intercourse with this cousin by brevet may not have been especially brilliant or of a nature calculated to be particularly interesting to other people, but to him it had been extremely agreeable, without doubt.

"Mornin' Mas' Robert," said Phil, as Robert passed the place at which the old negro was working. "How is ye dis mornin'?"

"Good morning, Phil. I am very well, I thank you. How are you, Phil?"

"Poorly, thank God. Ha! ha! ha! Dat's de way Bro' Joe and all de folks always says it. Dey never will own up to bein' rale well. But I tell ye now Mas' Robert, Phil's a well nigger al*ways*. I keeps up my eend de row all de time. I kin knock de spots out de work all day, daunce jigs till two o'clock, an' go 'possum huntin' till mornin' comes. Is ye ever been 'possum huntin', Mas' Robert?"

"No; I believe I never hunted opossums, but I should greatly like to try it, Phil."

"Would ye? Gim me yer han' Mas' Robert. You jes set de time now, and if Phil don't show you de sights o' 'possum huntin' you ken call me a po' white folkses nigger. Dat's a fac'."

Robert promised to make the necessary appointment in due time, and was just starting off again on his tramp, when Phil asked:

"Whare ye boun' dis mornin', Mas' Robert?"

"I'm going over to dine at The Oaks, Phil."

"Yer jest out de house in time. Dar comes Mas' Charles Harrison."

"I do not understand you, Phil. Why do you say I am out of the house just in time?"

"Mas' Robert, is you got two good eyes? Mas' Charles is a doctor you know, but dey a'n't nobody sick at Shirley. May be he's afraid Miss Sudie's gwine to get sick. Hi! git up Roley! dis a'n't plowin' mauster's field: g'long I tell ye!"

As Phil turned away Dr. Harrison rode up.

"Good morning, Mr. Pagebrook. On your way to The Oaks?"

"I was, but if you are going to Shirley I will walk back with you!"

"O no! no! I am only going to stop there a moment. I am on my way to see some patients at Exenholm, and as I had to go past Shirley I brought the mail, that's all. I'll not be there ten minutes, and I know they're expecting you at The Oaks. I brought Ewing along with me from the Court House. Foggy had been too much for him again."

"Why the boy promised me he would not gamble again."

"Oh! it's hardly gambling. Only a little game of loo. Every gentleman plays a little. I take a hand myself, now and then; but Foggy is a pretty old bird, you know, and he's too much for your cousin. Ewing oughtn't to play with *him*, of course, and that's why I brought him away with me. By the way, we're going to get a fox up in a day or two and show you some sport. The tobacco's all cut now, and the dogs are in capital order—as thin as a lath. You must be with us, of course. We'll get up one in pine quarter, and he's sure to run towards the river ; so you can come in as the hounds pass Shirley."

" I should like to see a fox hunt, certainly, but I have no proper horse," said Robert. '

" Why, where's Graybeard ? Billy told me he had turned him over to you to use and abuse."

" So he did, and he is riding his bay at present. But Graybeard is quite lame just now."

" Ride the bay then. Billy will be back from court to-night, won't he ? "

" Yes ; but he will want to join in the chase, I suppose."

" I reckon he will, but he can ride something else. He don't often care to take the tail, and he can see as much as he likes on one of his ' conestogas.' I'll tell you what you can do. Winger's got a splendid colt, pretty well broken, and you can get him for a dollar or two if you a'n't afraid to ride him. You must manage it somehow, so as to be ' in at the death !' I want you to see some riding."

Mr. Robert promised to see what he could do. He greatly wanted to ride after the hounds for once at least, though it must be confessed he would have been better pleased had the hounds to be ridden after belonged to somebody else besides the gentleman familiarly known as "Foggy," a personage for whom Mr. Robert had certainly not conceived a very great liking. That the reader may know whether his prejudice was a well-founded one or not it will be necessary for me to go back a little and gather up some of the loose threads of my story, while our young man is on his way to The Oaks. I have been so deeply interested in the ripening acquaintanceship between Mr. Rob and Miss Sudie that I have neglected to introduce some other personages, less agreeable perhaps, but not less important to the proper understanding of this history. Leaving young Pagebrook on the road, therefore, let me tell the reader, in a new chapter, something about the people he had met outside the hospitable Shirley mansion.

## CHAPTER X.

*Chiefly Concerning "Foggy."*

DR. CHARLES HARRISON was a young man of twenty-five or six, a distant relative of the Barksdales—so distant indeed that he would never have known himself as a relative at all, if he and they had not been Virginians. He was a young man of good parts, fond of field sports, reasonably well behaved in all external matters, but without any very fixed moral principles. He was a gentleman, in the strict Virginian sense of the term. That is to say he was of a good family, was well educated, and had never done anything to disgrace himself; wherefore he was received in all gentlemen's houses as an equal. He drank a little too freely on occasion, and played bluff and loo a trifle too often, the elderly people thought; but these things, it was commonly supposed, were only youthful follies. He would grow out of them—marry and settle down after awhile. He was on the whole a very agreeable person to be with, and very much of a gentleman in his manner.

"Foggy" Raves was an anomaly. His precise position in the social scale was a very difficult thing to discover, and is still more difficult to define. His father had been an overseer, and so " Foggy " was certainly not a " gentleman." Other men of parentage similar to his knew their places, and when business made it necessary for them to visit the house of a gentleman they expected to be received in the porch if the weather were tolerable, and in the dining-room if it were not. They never dreamed of being taken into the parlor, introduced to the family, or invited to dinner. All these things were well recognized customs; the line of demarkation between " gentlemen " and " common people " was very sharply drawn indeed. The two classes lived on excellent terms with each other, but they never mixed. The gentleman was always courteous to the common people out of respect for himself; while the common people were very deferential to every gentleman as a matter of duty. Now this man Raves was not a " gentleman." That much was clear. And yet, for some inscrutable reason, his position among the people who knew him was not exactly that of a common man. He was never invited into gentlemen's houses precisely as a gentleman would have been, it is true; and yet into gentlemen's houses he very often went, and that upon invitation too. When young men happened to be keeping bachelors' establishments, either temporarily or permanently, " Foggy " was sure to be invited pretty frequently to see them. As long as there were no ladies at home " Foggy " knew himself welcome, and he had played whist and loo and bluff in many genteel parlors, into which he never thought of going when there were ladies on the plantation. He kept a fine pack of hounds too, and was clearly at the head of the "fox-hunting interest" of the county; and this was an anomaly also, as fox-hunting is an eminently aristocratic sport, in which gentlemen engage only in company with gentlemen—except in "Foggy's" case.

Precisely what "Foggy's" business was it is difficult to say. He was constable, for one thing, and *ex-officio* county jailor. One half the jail building was fitted up as his residence, and there he lived, a bachelor some fifty years old. He hired out horses and buggies in a small way now and then, but his earnings were principally made at "bluff" and "loo." Once or twice Colonel Barksdale and some other gentlemen had tried to oust "Foggy" from the jail, believing that his establishment there was ruining a good many of the young men, as it certainly was. Failing in this they had him indicted for gambling in a public place, but the prosecution failed, the court holding that the jailor's private rooms in the jail could not be called a public place, though all rooms in a hotel had been held public within the meaning of the statute.

This man's Christian name was not "Foggy," of course, though hardly anybody knew what it really was. He had won his sobriquet in early life by paying the professional gambler, Daniel K. Foggy, to teach him "how to beat roulette," and then winning his money back by putting his purchased knowledge to the proof at Daniel's own roulette table. Everybody agreed that "Foggy" was a good fellow. He would go far out of his way to oblige anybody, and, as was pretty generally agreed, had a good many of the instincts of a gentleman. He was

"FOGGY."

73

not a professional gambler at all. He never kept a faro bank. He played cards merely for amusement, he said, and there was a popular tendency to believe his statement. The betting was simply to "make it interesting," and sometimes the play did grow very "interesting" indeed— interesting to the extent of several hundred dollars frequently.

Now only about a week before the morning on which Mr. Robert met Dr. Harrison, he had gone to the Court House for the purpose of calling upon the doctor. While there young Harrison had proposed that they go up to Foggy's, explaining that Foggy was "quite a character, whom you ought to know; not a gentleman, of course, but a good fellow as ever lived."

Upon going to Foggy's, Robert had found his cousin Ewing Pagebrook there playing cards. The boy—for he was not yet of age—was flushed and excited, and Robert saw at a glance that he had been losing heavily. On Robert's entrance he threw down his cards and declared himself tired of play.

"I'll arrange that, Foggy," said the boy, with a nod.

"O any time will do!" replied the other. "How d'ye do, Charley? Come in."

Dr. Charley introduced Robert, and the latter, barely recognizing Foggy's greeting, turned to Ewing and asked:

"What have you been doing, Ewing? Not gambling, I hope."

"O no! certainly not," said Foggy; "only a little game of draw-poker, ten cents ante."

"Well, but how much have you lost, Ewing?" asked

Robert. "How much more than you can pay in cash, I mean ? I see you haven't settled the score."

Ewing was inclined to resent his cousin's questioning, but his rather weak head was by no means a match for his cousin's strong one. This great hulking Robert Pagebrook was "big all over," Billy Barksdale had said. His will was law to most men when he chose to assert it strongly. He now took his cousin in hand, and made him confess to a debt of fifty dollars to the gambler. Then turning to Foggy he said :

"Mr. Raves, you have won all of this young man's money and fifty dollars more, it appears. Now, as I understand the matter, this fifty dollars is 'a debt of honor,' in gambling parlance, and so it must be paid. But you must acknowledge that you are more than a match for a mere boy, and you ought to 'give him odds.' I believe that is the correct phrase, is it not ?"

"Yes, that's right ; but how can you give odds in draw-poker ?"

"I am going to show you, though I am certainly not acquainted with the mysteries of that game. You and he think he owes you fifty dollars. Now my opinion is that he owes you nothing, while you owe him the precise amount of cash you have won from him ; and I propose to effect a compromise. The law of Virginia is pretty stringent, I believe, on the subject of gambling with people under age, and if I were disposed I could give you some trouble on that score. But I propose instead to pay you ten dollars—just enough to make a receipt worth while—and to take your receipt in full for the amount due. I shall then take my cousin home, and he can pay me at his leisure. Is that satisfactory, sir?"

Mr. Robert was in a towering rage, though his manner was as quiet as it is possible to conceive, and his voice was as soft and smooth as a woman's. Had Foggy been disposed to presume upon his antagonist's apparent calmness and to play the bully, he would unquestionably have got himself into trouble of a physical sort there and then. To speak plainly, Robert Pagebrook was quite prepared to punish the gambler with his fists, and would undoubtedly have made short work of it had Foggy provoked him with a word. But Foggy never quarreled. He knew his business too well for that. He never gave himself airs with gentlemen. He knew his place too well. He never got himself involved in any kind of disturbance which would attract attention to himself. He knew the consequences too well. He was always quiet, always deferential, always satisfied; and so, while he had no reason to anticipate the thrashing which Robert Pagebrook was aching to give him, he nevertheless was as complacent as possible in his reply to that gentleman.

"Why certainly, Mr. Pagebrook. I never meant to take the money at all. I only wanted to frighten our young friend here, and teach him a lesson. He thinks he can play cards when he can't, and I wanted to ' break him of sucking eggs,' that's all. I meant to let him think he had to pay me so as to scare him, for I feel an interest in Ewing.. 'Pon my word I do. Now let me tell you, Ewing, we'll call this square, and you mustn't play no more. You play honest now, but if you keep on you'll cheat a little after awhile, and when a man cheats at cards, Ewing, he'll steal. Mind, I speak from experience, for I've seen a good deal of this thing. Come, Charley, you and Mr. Pagebrook, let's take something. I've got some splendid Shield's whisky."

Mr. Pagebrook summoned sufficient courtesy to decline the alcoholic hospitality without rudeness, and, with his cousin, took his leave.

Ewing entreated Robert to keep the secret he had thus stumbled upon, and Robert promised to do so upon the express condition that Ewing would wholly refrain from playing cards for money in future. This the youth promised to do, and our friend Robert congratulated himself upon his success in saving his well-meaning but rather weak-headed cousin from certain ruin.

## CHAPTER XI.

### *Mr. Pagebrook Rides.*

IN view of the circumstances detailed in the preceding chapter, it was quite natural that Robert Pagebrook should feel some annoyance when he learned from young Harrison that his cousin had again fallen into the hands of Foggy Raves. And he did feel annoyance, and a good deal of it, as he resumed his walk toward The Oaks. Aside from his interest in his cousin, Robert disliked to be beaten at anything, and to find that the gambler had fairly beaten him in his fight for the salvation of Ewing was anything but agreeable to him. Then again his cousin had shown himself miserably weak of moral purpose, and weaknesses were always unpleasant things for Robert Pagebrook to contemplate. He had no sympathy with irresolution of any sort, and no patience with unstable moral knees. He was half angry and wholly grieved, therefore, when he heard of Ewing's violation of his promise. His first impulse was to go before the next grand jury and secure Foggy's indictment for gambling with a minor, but a maturer reflection convinced him that while this would be an agreeable thing to do under

the circumstances, it would be an unwise one as well.
To expose Ewing was to ruin him hopelessly, Robert felt,
knowing as he did that reformation in the face of public
disgrace requires a good deal more of moral stàmina than
Ewing Pagebrook ever had.    Precisely what to do Robert
did not know.    He would talk with Cousin Sudie about
the matter, and see what she thought was best.    Her
judgment, he had discovered, was particularly good, and
it might help him to a determination.

This thinking of Cousin Sudie brought back to his mind
Phil's hint as to the purpose of Dr. Harrison's visit, and
his face burned as the conviction came to him that this
man might be Cousin Sudie's accepted or acceptable lover.
He knew well enough that Harrison called frequently at
Shirley ; but surely Cousin Sudie would have mentioned
the man often in conversation if he had been largely
in her mind.    Would she though ?    This was a second
thought.    Was not her silence, on the contrary, rather
an indication that she did think of the man ?    If she recognized him as a lover, would she not certainly avoid all
unnecessary mention of his name ?    Was not Phil likely
to be pretty well informed in the case ?    All these
things ran rapidly through his perturbed mind.    But why
should he worry himself over a matter that in no way
concerned him ?    *He* was not interested in Cousin Sudie
except as a friend.    Of course not.    Was not his heart
still sore from its suffering at the hands of Miss Nellie
Currier ?    No ; upon the whole he was forced to confess
that it was not.    In truth he had not thought of that
young lady for at least a fortnight ; and now that he did

think of her he could not possibly understand how or why he had ever cared for her at all. But he was not in love with Cousin Sudie. Of that he wa. certain. And yet he could not avoid a feeling of very decided annoyance at the thought suggested by Phil's remark. He knew young Harrison very slightly, but he was accustomed to take men's measures pretty promptly, and he was not at all satisfied with this one as a suitor for Cousin Sudie. He knew that Foggy was the young physician's pretty constant associate. He knew that Harrison drank at times to excess, and he felt that he was not over scrupulous upon nice points of morality. In short, our young man was in a fair way to work himself into a very pretty indignation when he met Maj. Pagebrook's overseer, Winger. A negotiation immediately ensued, ending in an agreement that Robert should ride the black colt so long as Graybeard's lameness should continue, paying Winger a moderate hire for the animal.

The bargain concluded, Winger dismounted and Robert took his place on the colt's back, borrowing Winger's saddle until his return to Shirley in the evening.

Horseback exercise is a curious thing, certainly, in some of its effects. When Robert was afoot that morning several things had combined, as we have seen, to make him gloomy, despondent, and generally out of sorts. Ewing's backsliding had annoyed him, and the possibility or probability of Phil's accuracy of information and judgment in the matter of Cousin Sudie and Dr. Harrison had depressed him sorely. When he found himself on

the back of this magnificent colt, whose delight it was to
carry a strong, fearless rider, he fell immediately into
hearty sympatl y with the high spirits and bounding
pulses of the animal.  He struck out into a gallop, and
in an instant felt himself in a far brighter world than
that which he had been traversing ten minutes since.
His spirits rose.  His hopefulness returned.  The world
became better and the future more promising.  Mr.
Robert Pagebrook felt the unreasonable but thoroughly
delightful exhilaration to which Billy Barksdale referred
when he said, " Bob is the happiest fellow in the world ;
he gets glad sometimes just because he is alive."  That
was precisely the state of affairs.  Mr. Robert on this
high-mettled horse was superlatively alive, and was glad
because of it.  There is more of joy than many people
know in the mere act of living ; but it is only they who
have clear consciences, springy muscles, and perfect
health of both mind and body who fully share this joy.
Robert Pagebrook had all of these, and was astride a perfect horse to boot ; and that, as all horsemen know, is
an important element in the matter.

He galloped on toward The Oaks, leaving his troubles
just where he mounted his horse.  He forgot Ewing's
apostasy ; he forgot Dr. Harrison, but he remembered
Cousin Sudie, and that right pleasantly too.  Naturally
enough, being on horseback, he projected himself into the
future, which is always a bright world when one is galloping toward it.  He would heartily enjoy the coming
fox-chase—particularly on such an animal as that now
under him.  Then his thoughts pushed themselves still

further forward, and he dreamed dreams. His full professorship would pay him a salary sufficient to justify him in setting up a little establishment of his own, and he should then know what it was to have a home in which there should be love and purity and peace and domestic comfort. The woman who was to form the center of all this bliss was vaguely undefined as to identity and other details. She existed only in outline, in the picture, but that outline strikingly resembled the young woman who carried the key-basket at Shirley—an accidental resemblance, of course, for Mr. Robert Pagebrook was positive that he was not in love with Cousin Sudie.

## CHAPTER XII.

*Mr. Pagebrook Dines with his Cousin Sarah Ann.*

HOW largely Mr. Robert's high spirits were the result of rapid riding on a good horse, and how far
other causes aided in producing them, I am wholly unprepared to say. Whatever their cause was they were
not destined to last long after he dismounted at The Oaks.
Indeed his day at that country seat was not at all an
agreeable one. His cousin Sarah Ann was a rather de-
pressing person to be with at any time, and there were
circumstances which made her especially so on this particular occasion. Cousin Sarah Ann had a chronic habit
of being ostentatiously sorry for herself, which was very
disagreeable to a healthy young man like Robert. She
nursed and cherished her griefs as if they had been her
children, and like children they grew under the process.
She had several times told Robert how lonely she was
since the death of her mother, three years before, and
with tears in her eyes she had complained that there was
nobody to love her now that poor mother was gone—a
statement which right-thinking and logical Robert felt
himself almost guilty in hearing from a woman with a

husband and a house full of children. She complained a
good deal of her poverty, too, a complaining which
shocked this truthful young man, knowing, as he did,
that his cousin Edwin was one of the wealthiest men in
the country round about, with a good plantation at home,
a very large and profitable one in Mississippi, twenty or
thirty business buildings, well leased, in Richmond, a
surplus of money in bank, and no debts whatever, which
last circumstance served to make him almost a curiosity
in a state in which it was hardly respectable to owe no
money. She complained, too, that her boys were dull
and her girls not pretty, both of which complaints were
very well founded indeed. When Robert on his first visit
said something in praise of her comfortable and really
pretty house, she replied :

"Oh ! I can't pretend to live in an aristocratic house
like your Aunt Mary's. I didn't inherit a 'family mansion' you know, and so we had to build this house. It
hasn't a bit of wainscoting, you see, and no old pictures.
I reckon I a'n't as good as you Pagebrooks, and somehow
my husband a'n't as aristocratic as the rest of you. I
reckon he's only a half-blood Pagebrook, and that's why
he condescended to marry poor me."

This was Cousin Sarah Ann's favorite way of speaking of herself, and she said "poor me" with a degree of
pathos in her tone which always brought tears to her eyes.

On the present occasion, as I have said, there were circumstances which enabled this estimable lady to make
herself unusually disagreeable. She had a fresh affliction,
and so she reveled in an ecstasy of woe. It was her ambi-

tion in life to be exceptionally miserable, and accordingly
she welcomed sorrow with a keenness of relish which few
people can possibly know. She wouldn't be happy in
heaven, Billy Barksdale said, unless she could convince
people there that she was snubbed by the saints and put
upon by the angels.

When Robert arrived at The Oaks that morning Major
Pagebrook met him at the gate, according to custom, but
without his customary cheerfulness of countenance. He
offered no explanation, however, and Robert asked no
questions. The two went into the parlor, Robert catching sight of Ewing in the orchard back of the house, but
having no opportunity to speak to the young man.

Robert had not been in the parlor many minutes before
Major Pagebrook went out and Cousin Sarah Ann entered
and greeted him with her handkerchief to her eyes. She
made one or two ostentatious efforts to control herself,
and then ostentatiously burst into tears.

"Oh! Cousin Robert, I didn't mean to betray myself
this way. But I'm so miserable. Ewing has been led
away again by that man, Foggy Raves."

"I am heartily sorry to know it, Cousin Sarah Ann,"
replied Robert. "Did he lose much?"

"O Ewing never gambles! I don't mean that. Thank
heaven my boy never plays cards, except with small stakes
for amusement. But he went over to the Court House
last night to stay with Charley Harrison, and they went
up to Foggy's and they drank a little too much. And
now Cousin Edwin (Mrs. Pagebrook always called her
husband Cousin Edwin) is terribly angry about it and

COUSIN SARAH ANN.

has scolded the poor boy cruelly, cruelly. He even
threatened to cut him off with nothing at all in his will,
and leave the poor boy to starve. Men are *so* hard-hearted!
The idea that I should live to hear my boy talked to in
that way, and by his own father too, almost kills me.
Poor me ! there's nobody to love me now."

" Tell me, Cousin Sarah Ann," said Robert, " for I am
deeply concerned in Ewing's behalf, and I mean to reform
him if I can—does he often get drunk ?"

" Get drunk ! My boy never gets drunk ! You talk
just like Cousin Edwin. He only drinks a little, as all
young gentlemen do, and if he drinks too much now and
then I'm sure it isn't so very dreadful as you all make it
out. I don't see why the poor boy must be kept down all
the time and scolded and scolded and talked about, just
because he does like other people ; and that's what dis-
tresses me. Cousin Edwin scolds Ewing, and then scolds
me for taking the poor boy's part, and it's more than I
can bear. And now you talk about 'reforming' him !"

Robert explained that he had misunderstood the cause
of Cousin Sarah Ann's grief, but he thought it would be
something worse than useless to tell her that she was
ruining the boy, as he saw clearly enough that she was.
He turned the conversation, therefore, and Cousin Sarah
Ann speedily dried her eyes.

" You're riding Mr. Winger's horse, I see. What's
become of Graybeard ?" she asked, after a little time.

" He is a little lame just now. Nothing serious, but I
thought I would hire Winger's colt until he gets well."

" Ah ! I understand. The rides soon in the morning

must not be given up on any terms. But you'd better look out, Cousin Robert. I'm sorry for you if you lose your heart there."

"Why, Cousin Sarah Ann, what do you mean? I really am not sure that I understand you."

"Oh! I say nothing; but those rides every morning and all that housekeeping that I've heard about, are dangerous things, cousin. I was a belle once myself."

It was one of Cousin Sarah Ann's favorite theories that she knew all about bellehood, having been a belle herself —though nobody else ever knew anything about that particular part of her career.

"Well, Cousin Sarah Ann, I do not think I have lost my heart, as you phrase it; but pray tell me why you should be sorry for me if I had?"

Mr. Robert was at first about to declare positively that he had not fallen in love with Cousin Sudie, but just at that moment it occurred to him that he might possibly be mistaken about the matter, and being thoroughly truthful he chose the less positive form of denial, supplementing it, as we have seen, with a question.

"Well, for several reasons," replied Cousin Sarah Ann: "they do say that Charley Harrison is before you there, and anyhow, it would never do. Sudie hasn't got much, you know. Her father didn't leave her anything but a few hundred dollars, and that's all spent long ago, on her clothes and schooling."

Mr. Robert Pagebrook certainly did not wish ill to Cousin Sudie, and yet he was heartily though illogically glad when he learned that that young lady was poor.

The feeling surprised him, but he had no time in which to analyze it just then.

"Why, Cousin Sarah Ann, you certainly do not think me so mercenary as your remark would seem to indicate ?"

"Oh ! it's well enough to talk about not being mercenary, but I can tell you that some money on one side or the other is very convenient. I know by experience what it is to be poor. I might have married rich if I'd wanted to, but I had lofty notions like you."

The reader will please remember that I am no more responsible for Mrs. Pagebrook's syntax than for her sins.

"But, Cousin Sarah Ann," said Robert, "you would not wish one to marry a young woman's money or lands, would you ?"

"That's only your romantic way of putting it. I don't see why you can't love a rich girl as well as a poor one, for my part. If you had plenty of money yourself it wouldn't matter ; but as it is you ought to marry so as to hang up your hat."

"I confess I do not exactly understand your figure of speech, Cousin Sarah Ann ! What do you mean by hanging up my hat ?"

"Didn't you ever hear that before ? It's a common saying here, when a man marries a girl with a good plantation and a 'dead daddy,' so there can't be any doubt about the land being her's—they say he's got nothing to do but walk in and hang up his hat."

This explanation was lucid enough without doubt, but it, and indeed the entire conversation, was extremely disagreeable to Robert, who was sufficiently old-fashioned to think that marriage was a holy thing, and he, being a man of good taste, disliked to hear holy things lightly spoken of. He was relieved, therefore, by Maj. Page-brook's entrance, and not long afterwards he was invited to go up to the blue-room, the way to which he knew perfectly well, to rest awhile before dinner.

In the blue-room he found Ewing, with a headache, lying on a lounge. The youth had purposely gone thither, probably, in order that his meeting with Robert might be a private one, for meet him he must, as he very well knew, at dinner if not before.

Robert sat down by him and held his head as tenderly as a woman could have done, and speaking gently said :

"I am very sorry to find you suffering, Ewing. You must ride with me after dinner, and the air will relieve your head, I hope."

The boy actually burst into tears, and presently, recovering from the paroxysm, said :

"I didn't expect that, Cousin Robert. Those are the first kind words I've heard to-day. Mother has called me hard names all the morning."

"Your *mother!*" exclaimed Robert, thrown off his guard by surprise, for he would never have thought of questioning the boy on such a subject.

"O yes! she always does. If she'd ever give me any credit when I do try to do right, I reckon I would try harder. But she calls me a drunkard and gambler when-ever there is the least excuse for it; and if I don't do any-thing wrong she says I am pokey and a'n't got any spirit. She told me this morning she didn't mean to leave me anything in her will, because I'd squander it. You know all pa's property is in her name now. I got mad at last and told her I knew she couldn't keep me from getting my share, because nearly half of everything here belonged to Grandfather Taylor and is willed to us children when we come of age. She didn't know I knew that, and when I told her——"

"Come, Ewing, don't talk about that. You have no right to tell me such things. Bathe your head now, and hold it up as a man should. You are responsible to yourself for yourself, and it is your duty to make a man of yourself—such a man as you need not be ashamed of. If you think you do not receive the recognition you ought for your efforts to do well, you should remember that things are not perfectly adjusted in this world, so far at least as we can understand them. The reward of manliness is the manliness itself; and it is well worth living for too, even though nobody recognizes its existence but yourself. Of that, however, there need be no fear. People will know you, sooner or later, precisely as you are."

Robert had other encouraging things to say to the youth, and finally said:

"Now, Ewing, I shall ask you to make no promises which you may not be strong enough to keep; but if you will promise me to make an earnest effort to let whisky and cards alone, and to make a man of yourself, refusing to be led by other people, I will talk with your father and get him to agree never to mention the past again, but to aid you with every encouragement in his power for the future."

" Why, Cousin Robert, pa never says anything to me. When ma scolds he just goes out of the house, and he don't come in again till he's obliged to. It a'n't pa at all, it's ma, and it a'n't any use to talk to her. I'll be of age pretty soon, and then I mean to take my share of grandpa's estate, and put it into money and go clear away from here."

Robert saw that it would be idle to remonstrate with the young man at present, and equally idle to interfere with the domestic governmental system practiced by Cousin Sarah Ann. He devoted himself, therefore, to the task of getting Ewing to bathe his head ; and after a little time the two went down to dinner, Ewing thinking Robert the only real friend he could claim.

His head aching worse after dinner than before, he declined Robert's invitation to go to Shirley, and our friend rode back alone.

# CHAPTER XIII.

*Concerning the Rivulets of Blue Blood.*

MR. ROBERT was heartily glad to get away from the uncomfortable presence of Cousin Sarah Ann, and yet it can not be said that our young gentleman was buoyant of spirit as he rode from The Oaks to Shirley. Ewing's case had depressed him, and Cousin Sarah Ann had depressed him still further. His confidence in woman nature was shaken. His ideas on the subject of women had been for the most part evolved—wrought out, *a priori*, from his mother as a premise. He had known all the time that not every woman was his mother's equal, if indeed any woman was; he had observed that sometimes vanity and weakness and in one case, as we know, faithlessness entered into the composition of women, but he had never conceived of such a compound of "envy, hatred and malice, and all uncharitableness" as his cousin Sarah Ann certainly was; and as he applied the quotation mentally he was constrained also to utter the petition which accompanies it in the litany—"Good Lord deliver us!" This woman was a mystery to him. She not only

shocked but she puzzled him. How anybody could consent to be just such a person as she was was wholly in-
comprehensible. Her departures from the right line of
true womanhood were so entirely purposeless that he
could trace them to no logical starting-point. He could
conceive of no possible training or experience which ought
to result in such a character as hers.

After puzzling himself over this human problem for
half an hour he gave it up, and straightway began to work
at another. He asked himself how it could be possible
that Cousin Sudie should be attracted by Dr. Charley
Harrison. Possibly the reader has had occasion to work
at a similar problem in his time, and if so I need not tell
him how incapable it proved of solution. Of the fact
Robert was now convinced, and the fact annoyed him.
It annoyed him too that he could not account for the
fact; and then it annoyed him still more to know that he
could be annoyed at all in the case, for he was perfectly
sure—or nearly so—that he was not himself in love with
his little friend at Shirley. And yet he felt a strange
yearning to battle in some way with young Harrison, and
to conquer him. He wanted to beat the man at something, it mattered little what, and to triumph over him.
But he did not allow himself even mentally to formulate
this feeling. If he had he would have discovered its injustice, and cast it from him as unworthy. His instinct
warned him of this, and so he refused to put his wish into
form lest he should thereby lose the opportunity of entertaining it.

With thoughts like these the young man rode home-

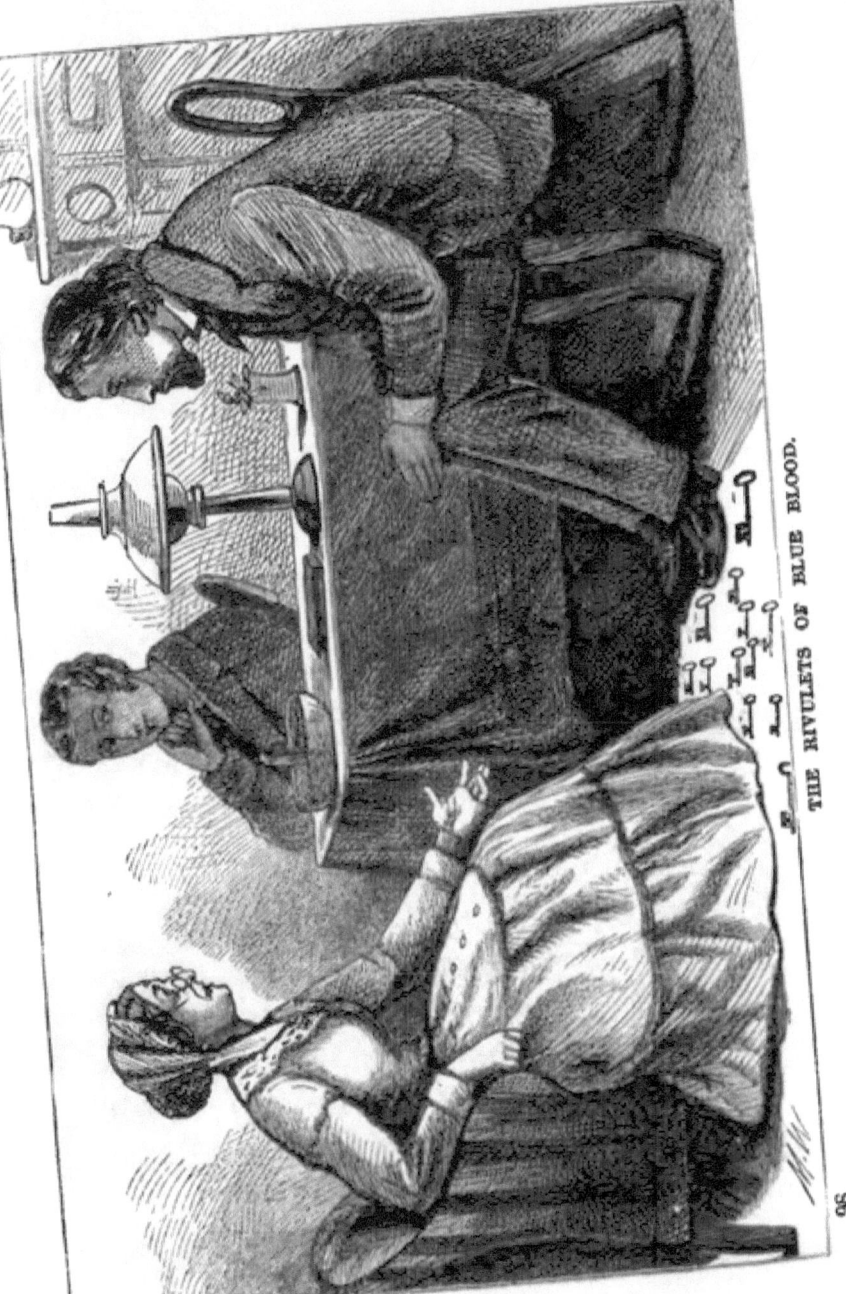

THE RIVULETS OF BLUE BLOOD.

wards, and naturally enough he was not in the best of humors when he sat down in the parlor at Shirley.

The conversation, in some inscrutable way, turned upon Cousin Sarah Ann, and Robert so far forgot himself as to express pleasure in the thought that that lady was in no way akin to himself.

"But she is kin to you, Robert," said Aunt Catherine.

"How can that be, Aunt Catherine?" asked the young gentleman.

"Show him with the keys, Aunt Catherine, show him with the keys," said Billy, who had returned from court that day. "Come, Sudie, where's your basket? I want to see if Aunt Catherine can't muddle Bob's head as badly as she does mine sometimes. Here are the keys. Explain it to him, Aunt Catherine, and if he knows when you get through whether he is his great grandfather's nephew or his uncle's son once removed, I'll buy his skull for tissue paper at once. A skull that can let key-basket genealogy through it a'n't thick enough to grow hair on."

The task was one that the old lady loved, and so without paying the slightest attention to Billy's bantering she began at once to arrange the keys from Sudie's basket upon the floor in the shape of a complicated genealogical table. "Now my child," said she, pointing to the great key at top, "the smoke-house key is your great great grandmother, who was a Pembroke. The Pembrokes were always considered——"

"Always considered smoke-house keys — remember, Bob."

"Will you keep still, William? The Pembrokes

were always considered an excellent family. Now your great great grandmother, Matilda Pembroke, married John Pemberton, and had two sons and one daughter, as you see. The oldest son, Charles, had six daughters, and his third daughter married your grandfather Pagebrook, so she was your grandmother—the store-room key, you see——"

"See, Bob, what it is to be well connected," said Billy; "your own dear grandmother was a store-room key."

"Hush, Billy, you confuse Robert."

"Ah! do I? I only wanted him to remember who his grandmother was."

"Well," said the old lady, "Matilda Pemberton's daughter, your great grand aunt, married a man of no family—a carpenter or something—the corn-house key there."

"There it is, Bob. A'n't you glad you descended from a respectable smoke-house key, through an aristocratic store-room key, instead of having a plebeian corn-house key in the way? There's nothing like blue blood, I tell you, and ours is as blue as an indigo bag; a'n't it, Aunt Catherine?"

"Will you never learn, Billy, not to make fun of your ancestors? I have explained to you a hundred times how much there is in family. Now don't interrupt me again. Let me see, where was I? O yes! Your great grand aunt married a carpenter, and his daughter Sarah was your second cousin if you count removes, fourth cousin if you don't. Now Sarah was your Cousin Sarah Ann's grandmother, as you see; so Sarah Ann is your third cousin if you count removes, and your sixth cousin if you don't. Do you understand it now?"

"Of course he does," said Billy; "but I must break up the family now, as I see Polidore's waiting for the madam's great grandfather, to wit, the corn-house key. Come Bob, let's go up to the stable and see the horses fed."

## CHAPTER XIV.

*Mr. Pagebrook Manages to be in at the Death.*

NOT many days after Robert's uncomfortable dinner at The Oaks, a servant came over with a message from Major Pagebrook, to the effect that a grand fox-chase was arranged for the next morning. Foggy and Dr. Harrison had originated it, but Major Pagebrook's and several other gentlemen's hounds would run, and Ewing invited his cousins, Robert and Billy, to take part in the sport. Accordingly our two young gentlemen ate an early breakfast and rode over to that part of The Oaks plantation known as "Pine quarter," where the first fox-hunt of the season was always begun. They arrived not a moment too soon, and found the hounds just breaking away and the riders galloping after them. The first five miles of country was comparatively open, a fact which gave the fox a good start and promised to make the chase a long and a rapid one.

Robert Pagebrook had never seen a fox-chase, and his only knowledge of the sport was that which he had gleaned from descriptions, but he was on a perfect horse

as inexperienced as himself; he was naturally very fearless; he was intensely excited, and it was his habit to do
whatever he believed to be the proper thing on any occasion. From books he had got the impression that the
proper thing to do in fox-hunting was to ride as hard as
he could straight after the hounds, and this he did with
very little regard for consequences. He galloped straight
through clumps of pine, "as thick," Billy said, "as the
hair on Absalom's head," while others rode around them.
He plunged through creek "low grounds" without a
thought of possible mires or quicksands. He knew that
fox-hunters made their horses jump fences, but he knew
nothing of their practice in the matter of knocking off
top rails first, and accordingly he rode straight at every
fence which happened to stand in his way, and forced his
horse to take them all at a flying leap.

On and on he went, straight after the hounds, his pulse
beating high and his brain whirling with excitement.
The more judicious hunters of the party would have been
left far behind but for the advantage they possessed in
their knowledge of the country and their consequent
ability to anticipate the fox's turnings, and to save dis-
tance and avoid difficulties by following short cuts. Robert rode right after the hounds always.

"That cousin of yours is crazy," said one gentleman
to Billy; "but what a magnificent rider he is."

"Why don't you stop your cousin?" asked another,
"he'll kill himself, to a certainty, if you don't."

"O I will!" replied Billy, "and I'll remonstrate with
all the streaks of lightning I happen to overtake, too.

I'm sure to catch a good many of them before I come up with him."

The fox "doubled" very little now, and it became evident that he was making for the Appomattox River, but whether he would cross it or double and run back was uncertain. Billy earnestly hoped he would double, as that might enable him to see Robert and check his mad riding, if indeed that gentleman should manage to reach the river with an unbroken neck.

On and on they went, fox running for dear life, hounds in perfect trim and full cry, and riders each bent upon "taking the tail" if possible. Robert remained in advance of all the rest, jumping every fence over which he could force his horse, and making the animal knock down those which he could not leap. His horse blundered at a ditch once and fell, but recovered himself with his rider still erect in the saddle, before anybody had time to wonder whether his neck was broken or not. Billy now saw a new danger ahead of his cousin. They were nearing the river, and the fox, an old red one, who knew his business, was evidently running for a crossing place where mire and quicksands abounded. Of this Robert knew nothing, and after his performances thus far there was no reason to hope that any late-coming caution would save him now. A thicket of young oaks lay just ahead, and the hounds going through it Robert followed quite as a matter of course. Billy saw here his chance, and putting spurs to his horse he rode at full speed around the end of the thicket, hoping to reach the other side in time to intercept his cousin, in whose behalf he was now really alarmed. As he swept by the end of the thicket, however, he passed two gentlemen whom he could not see through the bushes, but whose voices he knew very well. They were none other than Mr. Foggy Raves and Dr. Charles Harrison, and Billy heard what they were saying.

"You *must* take the tail, Charley, and not let that city snob get it. The fool rides like Death on the pale horse, and don't seem to know there ever was a fence too high to jump. He'd try to take the Blue Ridge at a flying leap if it got in his way. I'd rather kill a dozen horses than let him beat us. He put his finger into our little game with that saphead Ewing, and —— "

"But my horse is thumped now, Foggy."

"Well, take mine then. He's fresh. I sent him over last night to meet me here, and I just now changed. I've hurt my knee and can't ride. Take my horse and ride him to death but what you beat that —— "

This was all that Billy had time to hear, but it was enough to change his entire purpose. He no longer thought of Robert's neck, but hurried on for the sole purpose of spurring his cousin up to new exertion. He reached the edge of the thicket just as Robert came out bareheaded, having lost his hat in the brush. His face was bleeding, too, from scratches and bruises received in the struggle through the oak thicket. The river was just ahead, but the fox doubled to the right instead of crossing.

"Come, Bob," said Billy, "you've got to take the tail to-day or die. Foggy and Charley Harrison have been setting up a game on you, and Charley has a fresh horse,

borrowed from Foggy on purpose to beat you.    But this
double gives you a quarter start of him.    Don't *run* your
horse up hills, or you'll blow him out, and shy off from
such thickets as that.    You can ride round quicker than
you can go through.    *Don't break your* NECK, BUT TAKE
THE TAIL ANYHOW.

He fairly yelled the last words at Robert, who was already a hundred yards ahead of him and getting further
off every second.

The effect of his words on his cousin was not precisely
what might have been expected.    Before this Robert had
been intensely excited and had enjoyed being so, but his
excitement had been the result of his high spirits and
his keen zest for the sport in which he was engaged.    He
had astonished everybody by the utter recklessness of his
riding, but had not shared at all in their astonishment
or known that his riding was reckless.    He had ridden
hard simply because he thought that the proper thing to
do and because he enjoyed doing it.    He rode now for
victory.    His features lost the look of wild enjoyment
which they had worn, and settled themselves into a firm,
hard expression of dogged determination.    Here was his
opportunity to do battle with young Harrison; and from
Billy's manner, rather than from his words, he knew that
the contest was not one of generous rivalry on Harrison's
part.    He felt that there was a contemptuous sneer somewhere back of Billy's words, and the thought nettled him
sorely.    But he did not lose his head in the excitement.
On the contrary, he felt the necessity now for care and
coolness, and accordingly he immediately took pains to

become both cool and careful. He knew that Harrison
had an advantage in knowing the country, and he resolved to share that advantage. To this end he brought
his horse down to an easy canter and waited for Harrison
to come up. He then kept his eye constantly on his
rival and used him as a guide. When Harrison avoided a
thicket he avoided it also. If Harrison left the track of
the hounds for the sake of cutting off an angle, Robert
kept by his side. This angered Harrison, who had
counted confidently upon having an advantage in these
matters, and under the influence of his anger he spurred
his horse unnecessarily and soon took a good deal of his
freshness out of him.

The two rode on almost side by side for miles. The
fox was beginning to show his fatigue, and it was evident
that the chase would soon end. Both the foremost riders
discovered this, and both put forth every possible exertion
to win. Just ahead of them lay a very dense thicket
through which ran a narrow bridle-path barely wide
enough for one horse, as Robert knew, for the thicket lay
on Shirley plantation, the fox having run back almost
immediately over his own track. It was evident now that
"the catch" would occur in the field just beyond this
thicket, and it was equally evident that as the two could
not possibly ride abreast along the bridle-path, the one
who could first put his horse into it would almost certainly be first in at the death. They rode like madmen,
but Robert's horse was greatly fatigued and Harrison shot
ahead of him by a single length into the path. There was
hardly a chance for Robert now, as it was impossible in

any case for him to pass his rival in the thicket, and he could see that the dogs had already caught the fox in the field, less than a rod beyond its edge.

"I've got you now, I reckon," shouted Harrison looking back, but at the moment his horse stumbled and fell. Robert could no more stop his own horse than he could have stopped a hurricane, and the animal fell heavily over Harrison, throwing Robert about ten feet beyond and almost among the dogs. Getting up he ran in among the bellowing hounds and, catching the fox in his hand, he held him up in full view of the other gentlemen, now riding into the field from different directions and cheering as lustily as possible.

# CHAPTER XV.

## *Some very Unreasonable Conduct.*

QUITE naturally Robert was elated as he stood there bare-headed, and received the congratulations of his companions, who had now come up and gathered around him. Loudest among them was Foggy, who leaping from his horse cried out:

"By Jove, Mr. Pagebrook, I must shake your hand. I never saw prettier riding in my life, and I've seen some good riding too in my time. But where's your horse? Did you turn him loose when you jumped off?"

This served to remind Robert of the animal and of Harrison too, and going hastily into the thicket he found the Doctor repairing his girth, which had been broken in the fall. The Doctor was not hurt, nor was his horse injured in any way, but the black colt which had carried Robert so gallantly lay dead upon the ground. An examination showed that in falling he had broken his neck.

It was not far that our young friend had to walk to reach Shirley, but a weariness which he had not felt before crept over him as he walked. His head ached sorely, and as the excitement died away it was succeeded by a numbness of despondency, the like of which he had never known before. He had declined to "ride and tie" with Billy, thinking the task a small one to walk through by a woods path to the house, while Billy followed the main road. With his first feeling of despondency came bitter mortification at the thought that he had allowed so small a thing as a fox-chase to so excite him. The exertion had been well enough, but he felt that the object in view during the latter half of the chase, namely, the defeat of young Harrison, was one wholly unworthy of him, and the color came to his cheek as he thought of the energy he had wasted on so small an undertaking. Then he remembered the gallant animal sacrificed in the blind struggle for mere victory, and he could hardly force the tears back as the thought came to him in full force that the nostrils which had quivered with excitement so short a time since, would snuff the air no more forever. He felt guilty, almost of murder, and savagely rejoiced to know that the death of the horse would entail a pecuniary loss upon himself, which would in some sense avenge the wrong done to the noble brute.

The numbness and weariness oppressed him so that he sat down at the root of a tree, and remained there in a state of half unconsciousness until Billy came from the house to look for him. Arrived at the house he went immediately to bed and into a fever which prostrated him for nearly a week, during which time he was not allowed to talk much ; in point of fact he was not inclined to talk at all, except to Cousin Sudie, who moved quietly in and out of the room as occasion required and came to sit by his bedside frequently, after Billy and Col. Barksdale quitted home again to attend court in another of the adjoining counties, as they did as soon as Robert's physician pronounced him out of danger. At first Cousin Sudie was disposed to enforce the doctor's orders in regard to silence; but she soon discovered, quick-witted girl that she was, that *her* talking soothed and quieted the patient, and so she talked to him in a soft, quiet voice, securing, by violating the doctor's injunction, precisely the result which the injunction was intended to secure. As soon as the fever quitted him Robert began to recover very rapidly, but he was greatly troubled about the still unpaid-for horse.

Now he knew perfectly well that Cousin Sudie had no money at command, and he ought to have known that it was a very unreasonable proceeding upon his part to consult her in the matter. But love laughs at logic as well as at locksmiths, and so our logical young man very illogically concluded that the best thing to do in the premises was to consult Cousin Sudie.

"I am in trouble, Cousin Sudie," said he, as he sat with her in the parlor one evening, "about that horse. I know Mr. Winger is a poor man, and I ought to pay him at once, but the truth is I have hardly any money with me, and there is no bank nearer than Richmond at which to get a draft cashed."

"You have money enough, then, somewhere?" asked Cousin Sudie.

"O yes! I have money in bank in Philadelphia, but

Winger has already sent me a note asking immediate payment, and telling me he is sorely pressed for money; and I dislike exceedingly to ask his forbearance even for a week, under the circumstances."

"Why can't you get Cousin Edwin to cash a check for you?" asked the business-like little woman; "he always has money, and will do it gladly, I know."

"That had not occurred to me, but it is a good suggestion. If you will lend me your writing-desk I will write and —— "

"Ah, there comes Cousin Edwin now, and Ewing too, to see you," said Miss Sudie, hearing their voices in the porch.

The visitors came into the parlor, and after a little while Sudie withdrew, intent upon some household matter. Ewing followed her. Robert spoke frankly of his wish to pay Winger promptly, and asked:

"Can you cash my check on Philadelphia for me, Cousin Edwin, for three hundred dollars? Don't think of doing it, pray, if it is not perfectly convenient."

"O it isn't inconvenient at all," said Major Pagebrook. "I have more money at home than I like to keep there, and I can let you have the amount and send your check to the bank in Richmond and have it credited to me quite as well as not. In fact I'd rather do it than not, as it'll save expressage on money."

Accordingly Robert drew a check for three hundred dollars on his bankers in Philadelphia, making it payable to Major Pagebrook, and that gentleman undertook to pay the amount that evening to Winger. Shortly after

this business matter had been settled, Ewing and Miss
Sudie returned to the parlor and the callers took their
departure.

Robert and Sudie sat silent for some time watching the
flicker of the fire, for the days were cool now and fires
were necessary to in-door comfort. How long their silence might have continued but for an interruption, I do
not know; but an interruption came in the breaking of
the forestick, which had burned in two. A broken rev-
erie may sometimes be resumed, but a pair of broken rev-
eries never are. Had Mr. Robert been alone he would
have rearranged the fire and then sat down to his
thoughts again. As it was he rearranged the fire and
then began to talk with Miss Sudie.

"I am glad to get that business off my hands. It
worried me," he said.

"So am I," said his companion, "very glad indeed."

There must have been something in her tone, as there
was certainly nothing in her words, which led Mr. Pagebrook to think that this young lady's remark had an
unexpressed meaning back of it. He therefore question-
ed her.

"Why, Cousin Sudie? had it been troubling you too?"

"No; but it would have done so, I reckon."

"I do not understand you. Surely you never doubted
that I would pay for the horse, did you?"

"No indeed, but—"

"What is it Cousin Sudie? tell me what there is in
your mind. I shall feel hurt if you do not."

"I ought not to tell you, but I must now, or you will

imagine uncomfortable things. I know why Mr. Winger wrote you that note."

"You know why? There was some reason then besides his need of money?"

"He was not pressed for the money at all. That wasn't the reason."

"You surprise me, Cousin Sudie. Pray tell me what you know, and how."

"Well, promise me first that you won't get yourself into any trouble about it—no, I have no right to exact a blind promise—but do don't get into trouble. That detestable man, Foggy Raves, made Mr. Winger uneasy about the money. He told him you were 'hard up' and couldn't pay if you wanted to; and I'm glad you have paid him, and I'm glad you beat Charley Harrison in the fox-chase, too."

With this utterly inconsequent conclusion, Cousin Sudie commenced rocking violently in her chair.

"How do you know all this, Cousin Sudie?" asked Robert.

"Ewing told me this evening. I'd rather you'd have killed a dozen horses than to have had Charley Harrison beat you."

"Why, Cousin Sudie?"

"O he's at the bottom of all this. He always is. Foggy is his mouth-piece. And then he told Aunt Catherine, the day you went to The Oaks, that he 'meant to have some fun when he got you into a fox-hunt on Winger's colt.' He said you'd find out how much your handsome city riding-school style was worth when you got

MISS SUDIE DECLARES HERSELF "SO GLAD."

on a horse you were afraid of. I'm *so* glad you beat him !"

Now it would seem that Cousin Sudie's rejoicing must have been of a singular sort, as she very unreasonably burst into tears while in the very act of declaring herself glad.

Mr. Robert Pagebrook was wholly unused to the task of soothing a woman in tears. It was his habit, under all circumstances, to do the thing proper to be done, but of what the proper thing was for a man to do or say to a woman in tears without apparent cause, Mr. Robert Pagebrook had not the faintest conception, and so he very unreasonably proceeded to take her hand in his and to tell her that he loved her, a fact which he himself just then discovered for the first time.

Before he could add a word to the blunt declaration, Dick thrust his black head into the door-way with the announcement, "Supper's ready, Miss Sudie."

# CHAPTER XVI.

*What Occurred Next Morning.*

THE reader thinks, doubtless, that Master Dick's entrance at the precise time indicated in the last chapter was an unfortunate occurrence, and I presume Mr. Pagebrook was of a like opinion at the moment. But maturer reflection convinced him that the interruption was a peculiarly opportune one. He was a conscientious young man, and was particularly punctilious in matters of honor; wherefore, had he been allowed to complete the conversation thus unpremeditatedly begun, without an opportunity to deliberate upon the things to be said, he would almost certainly have suffered at the hands of his conscience in consequence. There were circumstances which made some explanations on his part necessary, and he knew perfectly well that these explanations would not have been properly made if Master Dick's interruption had not come to give him time for reflection.

All this he thought as he drank his tea; for when supper was announced both he and Miss Sudie went into the dining-room precisely as if their talk in the parlor had been of no unusual character. This they did because they were creatures of habit, as you and I and all the rest of mankind are. They were in the habit of going to supper when it was ready, and it never entered the thought of either to act differently on this particular occasion. Miss Sudie, it is true, ran up to her room for a moment—to brush her hair I presume—before she entered the dining-room, but otherwise they both acted very much as they always did, except that Robert addressed almost the whole of his conversation during the meal to his Aunt Mary and Aunt Catherine, while Miss Sudie, sitting there behind the tea-tray, said nothing at all. After tea the older ladies sat with Robert and Sudie in the parlor, until the early bed-time prescribed for the convalescent young gentleman arrived.

It thus happened that there was no opportunity for the resumption of the interesting conversation interrupted by Dick, until the middle of the forenoon next day. Miss Sudie, it seems, found it necessary to go into the garden to inspect some late horticultural operations, and Mr. Robert, quite accidentally, followed her. They discussed matters with Uncle Joe, the gardener, for a time, and then wandered off toward a summer-house, where it was pleasant to sit in the soft November sunlight.

The conversation which followed was an interesting one, of course. Let us listen to it.

"The vines are all killed by the frost," said Cousin Sudie.

"Yes; you have frosts here earlier than I thought," said Robert.

"O we always expect frost about the tenth of October;

at least the gentlemen never feel safe if their tobacco isn't cut by that time. This year frost was late for us, but the nights are getting very cool now, a'n't they?"

"Yes; I found blankets very comfortable even before the tenth of October."

"It's lucky then that you wa'n't staying with Aunt Polly Barksdale."

"Why? and who is your Aunt Polly?"

"Aunt Polly? Why she is Uncle Charles's widow. She is the model for the whole connection; and I've had her held up to me as a pattern ever since I can remember, but I never saw her till about a year ago, when she came and staid a week or two with us; and between ourselves I think she is the most disagreeably good person I ever saw. She *is* good, but somehow she makes me wicked, and I don't think I'm naturally so. I didn't read my Bible once while she staid, and I do love to read it. I suppose I shall like to have her with me in heaven, if I get there, because there I won't have anything for her to help me about, but here 'I'm better midout' her."

"I quite understand your feeling; but you haven't told me why I'm lucky not to have her for my hostess these cold nights."

"O you'd be comfortable enough now that tobacco is cut; but when Cousin Billy staid with her, a good many years ago, he used to complain of being cold—he was only a boy—and ask her for blankets, and she would hold up her hands and exclaim: 'Why, child, your uncle's tobacco isn't cut yet! It will never do to say it's cold enough for blankets when your poor uncle hasn't got his tobacco cut. Think of your uncle, child! he can't afford to have his tobacco all killed.' But come, Cousin Robert, you mustn't sit here ; besides I want to show you an experiment I am trying with winter cabbage."

This, I believe, is a faithful report of what passed between Robert and Sudie in the summer-house. I am very well aware that they ought to have talked of other things, but they did not; and, as a faithful chronicler, I can only state the facts as they occurred, begging the reader to remember that I am in no way responsible for the conduct of these young people.

The cabbage experiment duly explained and admired, Mr. Robert and Miss Sudie walked out of the garden and into the house. There they found themselves alone again, and Robert plunged at once into the matter of which both had been thinking all the time.

"Cousin Sudie," he said, "have you thought about what I said to you last night ? "

"Yes—a little."

" I will not ask you just yet *what* you have thought," said Robert, taking her unresisting hand into his, "because there are some explanations which I am in honor bound to make to you before asking you to give me an answer, one way or the other. When I told you I loved you, of course I meant to ask you to be my wife, but that I must not ask you until you know exactly what I am. I want you to know precisely what it is that I ask you to do. I am a poor man, as you know. I have a good position, however, with a salary of two thousand dollars a year, and that is more than sufficient for the support of a family, particularly in an inexpensive college town ; so that there is room for a little constant accumulation. If I marry, I shall insure my life for ten thousand dollars, so that my death shall not leave my wife destitute. I have a very small reserve fund in bank too— thirteen hundred dollars now, since I paid for that horse. And there is still three hundred dollars due me for last year's work. These are my means and my prospects, and now I tell you again, Sudie, that I love you, and I ask you bluntly will you marry me ?"

The young lady said nothing.

" If you wish for time to think about it Sudie—"

" I suppose that would be the proper way, according to custom; but," raising her eyes fearlessly to his, " I have already made up my mind, and I do not want to act a falsehood. There is nothing to be ashamed of, I suppose, in frankly loving such a man as you, Robert. I will be your wife."

The little woman felt wonderfully brave just then, and accordingly, without further ado, she commenced to cry.

The reader would be very ill-mannered indeed should he listen further to a conversation which was wholly private and confidential in its character ; wherefore let us close our ears and the chapter at once.

# CHAPTER XVII.

*In which Mr. Pagebrook Bids his Friends Good-by.*

THE next two or three days passed away very quickly with Mr. Robert and Miss Sudie. Robert made to his aunt a statement of the results, without entering into the details of his conferences with Miss Sudie, and was assured of Col. Barksdale's approval when that gentleman and Billy should return from the court they were attending. The two young people, however, were in no hurry for the day appointed for that return to come. They were very happy as it was. They discussed their future, and laid many little plans to be carried out after awhile. It was arranged that Robert should return to Virginia at the beginning of the next long vacation; that the wedding should take place immediately upon his coming; and that the two should make a little trip through the mountains and, returning to Shirley, remain there until the autumn should bring Robert's professional duties around again.

They were in the very act of talking these matters over for the twentieth time, one afternoon, when Maj. Pagebrook rode up. He seemed absent and nervous in manner, and after a few moments of general conversation asked to see Robert alone upon business. When the two were closeted together Maj. Pagebrook opened his pocketbook and taking out a paper he slowly unfolded it, saying: "I have just received this, Robert, and I suppose there is a duplicate of it awaiting you in the postoffice."

Robert looked at the paper in blank astonishment.

"What does this mean?" he cried; "my draft protested! Why I have sixteen hundred dollars in that bank, and my draft was for only three hundred."

"It appears that the bank has failed," said Maj. Pagebrook. "At least I reckon that's what the Richmond people mean. They say, in a note to me, that it 'went to pot' a week ago. It seems there are a good many banks failing this fall. I hope you won't lose everything, though, Robert."

The blow was a terrible one to the young man. In a moment he took in the entire situation. To lose the money he had in bank was to be forced to begin the world over again with absolutely nothing; but at any rate he could pay the debt he owed to his cousin very shortly, and to be free from debt is in itself a luxury to a man of his temperament. He thought but a moment and then said:

"Cousin Edwin, I shall have to ask you to carry that protested draft for me a few days if you will. There is some money due me on the fifteenth of this month, and it is now the ninth. I asked that it should be sent to me here, but I shall go to Philadelphia at once, and I'll collect it when I get there and send you the amount. I promise you faithfully that it shall be remitted by the fifteenth at the very furthest."

"O don't trouble yourself to be so exact, Robert," replied Maj. Pagebrook. "Send it when you can ; I'm in no very great hurry. Sarah Ann says we must invest all our spare money in the new railroad stock ; but I needn't pay anything on that till the twenty-third, so there will be time enough. But for that I wouldn't care how long I waited."

"I shall not let it remain unpaid after the fifteenth at furthest," said Robert. "I do not like to let it lie even that long."

Maj. Pagebrook took his departure and Robert told Sudie of the bad news, telling her also that he must leave next morning for Philadelphia, to see if it were possible to save something from the wreck of the bank.

"Besides," said he, "I must get to work. There are nearly two months of time between now and the first of January, and I cannot afford to lose it now that I have lost this money."

"What will you do, Robert ? You can't do anything teaching in that time."

"No, but I can do a good many things. I write a little now and then for the papers and magazines, for one thing. I can pick up something, I think, which will at least pay expenses."

He then told her of his arrangement with Maj. Pagebrook about the protested draft, and finished by repeat-

ing what that gentleman had said about the investment
in railroad stock.

This troubled Miss Sudie more than all the rest, and
Robert seeing it pressed her for a reason. But no reason
would she give, and Robert was forced to content himself
with the thought that his trouble naturally brought
trouble to her. To her aunt, however, she expressed her
conviction that Cousin Sarah Ann had suggested the
railroad investment merely for the sake of compelling
her husband to press Robert for payment. She was
troubled to know that the payment must be deferred even
for a few days, but rejoiced in the knowledge of Robert's
ability to discharge his indebtedness speedily. It galled
her to think of the unpleasant things which the amiable
mistress of The Oaks would manage to say about Robert
pending the payment. There was no help for it, however,
and so the brave little woman persuaded herself that it
was her duty to appear cheerful in order that Robert
might be so; and whatever Miss Sudie believed to be
her duty in any case Miss Sudie did, however difficult
the doing might be. She accordingly wore the pleasant-
est possible smile and the most cheerful of countenances
whenever Robert was present, doing every particle of her
necessary crying in her own room and carefully washing
away all traces of the process before opening the door.

Robert made all his preparations for departure that
afternoon, and on the following morning was driven to
the Court House in the family carriage. When he arrived there he got what letters there were for him in the
post-office, read them, and talked a few moments with

Ewing Pagebrook, who had spent the preceding night with Foggy and Dr. Harrison, and was now deeply contrite and rather anxious than otherwise that Robert should scold him. There was no time, however, even for the giving of advice, as the train had now come, and Robert must go at once. A hasty hand-shaking closed the interview, and Robert was gone.

## CHAPTER XVIII.

*Mr. Pagebrook Goes to Work.*

WHEN Robert arrived in Philadelphia his first care was to make inquiries with regard to the bank in which his money was deposited. He learned that it had suspended payment about one week before, and that its affairs were in the hands of an assignee. This was all he could find out on the afternoon of his arrival, and with this he was forced to content himself until the next day, when he succeeded with some little difficulty in securing an interview with the assignee. To him he said : "My only purpose is to ascertain the exact state of the bank's affairs, in order that I may know what to do."

"That I cannot tell you, sir. The books are still in confusion, and until they can be straightened out it is impossible to say what the result will be."

"Tell me, then, are the assets anything like equal to the liabilities ?"

"That is exactly what the books must show. I can't say till we get a statement."

"You can at least tell me then," said Robert, provoked at the man's reticence, "whether there are any assets at all, or not."

"No, I can make no statement until the books are examined. Then a complete exhibit of affairs will be made."

"Pardon me," said Robert, "but this question is one

of serious moment to me. You have been examining this bank's affairs for a week, I believe?"

"Yes, about a week."

"You must have some idea, then, whether or not there is likely to be anything at all left for depositors, and you will oblige me very much indeed by giving me your personal opinion on the subject. I understand how impossible it is to give exact figures; but you cannot have failed to discover by this time whether or not the assets amount to anything worth considering, as compared with the amount of the bank's liabilities. I would like the little information you can give me, however inexact it may be."

"My dear sir," said the assignee, "I'm afraid you don't understand these things. Our statement is not ready yet, and I can not possibly tell you what its nature will be until it is."

"When will it be ready, sir?" asked Robert.

"That I can not say as yet, but it will be forthcoming in due time, sir; in due time."

"Will it require a week, or a month, or two or three months? You can, at least, make an approximate estimate of the time necessary for its preparation."

"Well, no," said the man of business, "I should not like to make any promises; I am hard at work, and the statement will be ready in due time, sir; in due time."

Robert left the man's presence thoroughly disgusted. Thinking the matter over he concluded that the affairs of the bank must be in a very bad way. Otherwise, he argued, the man would not be so silent on the subject.

Now the assignee was perfectly right in saying that

Robert did not understand these things.   If he had
understood them he would have known that the reticence
from which he thus argued the worst, meant just nothing at all.   Business men are not apt to commit themselves unnecessarily in any case, and especially in such a
case as the one concerning which Robert had been inquir-
ing.   The bank might have been utterly bankrupt or
entirely solvent, and that assignee would in either case
have given precisely the same answers to our young
friend's questions.   He knew nothing with absolute certainty as yet, and could know nothing certainly until the
last column of figures should be added up and the final
balances struck.   Then he could make a statement, but
until then he would say nothing at all.   He acted after
his kind.   Business is business ; and, as a rule, business
men know only one way of doing things.

Robert, however, was not a business man.   He knew
nothing about these things, and accordingly, making no
allowance for a business habit as one of the factors in the
problem, he proceeded to argue that if the affairs of the
bank were in the least degree hopeful the man would
have said so.   As he had carefully and persistently avoided
saying anything of the kind, Robert could only conclude
that there was no hope at all to be entertained.

He quickly determined, therefore, to waste no more
time.   Abandoning his sixteen hundred dollars as utterly
lost, he packed his valise and went at once to New York
to find work of some kind.   How he succeeded we shall
best see from his letter to Cousin Sudie, from which I am
allowed to quote a passage or two.

"I am very busy with some topical articles, as the newspaper folk call them. That is to say, I am visiting factories of various kinds and writing detailed accounts of their operations, coupling with the facts gathered thus, a gossipy account of the origin, history, etc., of the industry. I find the work very interesting, and it promises to be quite remunerative too. I fell into it by accident. About a year ago I spent an evening with a friend, Mr. Dudley, in New York, and while at his house his seven year old boy showed me some of his toys—little German contrivances; and I, knowing something about the toys and the people who make them—you know I made a summer trip through Europe once—fell to telling him about them. His father was as much interested as he, but the matter soon passed from my mind. When I came over here a week ago to look for something to do I visited the office of this paper, hoping that I should be allowed to do a little reporting or drudgery of some sort till something better should turn up. Who should I find in the editor's chair but my friend Dudley. I told him my errand, and his reply was:

" 'I haven't a moment now, Pagebrook, but you're the very man I want; come up and see me this evening. We dine at half-past six, and over our roast-beef I can explain fully what I mean.'

"I went, as a matter of course, and at dinner Dudley said :

" 'Our paper, Pagebrook, is meant to be a kind of American Penny Magazine. That is to say, we want to fill it full of *entertaining* information, partly for the sake

of the information but more for the sake of the enter-
tainment.   Now I have tried at least fifty people, in the
hope of finding somebody who could tell, in writing, just
such things as you told our Ben when you were here a
year ago.   I never dreamed of getting you to do it, but
you're just the man, and about the only one, too, I begin
to think.   Now, if you've a mind to do it, I can keep
you busy as long as you like.   I don't mean to confine
you to this particular kind of work, but I'd rather have
articles of that sort than any others, and the publishers
won't grumble if I pay you twenty dollars apiece for
them.   They mustn't exceed two of our columns—say
two thousand words in all—but if you can't tell your
story in any particular instance within those limits, you
can make two articles out of it.   I've already told your
toy story, but you can easily hunt up plenty of other
things to tell about.   Common things are best—things
people see every day but know nothing about.'

"I set to work the next day, and have been busy ever
since.   I like to visit factories and learn all the petty details of their operations, and I find that it is the petty
details which go to make the description interesting.   I
like the work so well that I almost wish I had no professorship, so that I might follow as a business this kind of
writing, and some other sorts in which I seem to succeed
—for I do not confine myself to one class of articles, or
to one paper either, for that matter, but am trying my
hand at a variety of things, and I find the work very fas-
cinating.   But it is altogether better, I suppose, that I
should retain my position in the college, even if I could

be sure of always finding as good a market as I do just now for my wares, which is doubtful. I have lost the whole of my little reserve fund—as the bank seems hopelessly broken; and if I had nothing to depend upon except the problematic sale of articles, I would do you a wrong to ask you to let our wedding-day remain fixed. As it is, my salary from the college is more than sufficient for our support, and as my expenses from now until the time appointed will be very small indeed, I shall have several hundred dollars accumulated by that time; wherefore if Uncle Carter does not object, pray let our plans remain undisturbed, will you not, Sudie?"

The rest of this letter, which is a very long one, is not only personal in its character, but is also of a strictly private nature; and while I am free to copy here so much of this and other letters in my possession as will aid me in the telling of my story, I do not feel myself at liberty to let the reader into the sacred inner chambers of a correspondence with which we have properly no concern, except as it helps us to the understanding of this history.

# CHAPTER XIX.

*A Short Chapter, not very interesting, perhaps, but of some Importance in the Story, as the Reader will probably discover after awhile.*

WHEN the letter from which a quotation was made in the preceding chapter came to Miss Sudie, that young lady was not at Shirley but at The Oaks, where Ewing was lying very ill. He had been prostrated suddenly, a few days before, and from the first had been delirious with fever. The doctor had appeared unusually anxious regarding his patient ever since he was first summoned to see him, and Cousin Sarah Ann having given way to her alarm at the evident danger in which her son lay to such an extent as to be wholly useless to herself or to anybody else, Miss Sudie had been called in to act as temporary mistress of the mansion.

The very next mail after the one which brought her letter, had in it one from Robert addressed to Ewing himself. Miss Sudie, upon discovering it in the bag, carried it to Cousin Sarah Ann, and was very decidedly shocked when that estimable lady without a word broke the seal and read the letter, putting it carefully away afterwards in Ewing's desk, of which she had the key.

Miss Sudie said nothing, however, and the matter was almost forgotten when in the evening the doctor came and sat down by the sick boy's bed.

"I think it my duty to tell you," said he to Cousin Sarah Ann, "that the crisis of the disease is rapidly approaching, and I must wait here until it passes. Your son is in very great danger; but we shall know within a few hours whether there is hope for him or not. I confess that while I hope the best I fear the worst."

Mrs. Pagebrook was thoroughly overcome by her fright. She loved her son, in her own queer way; and being a very weak woman she gave way entirely when she understood in how very critical a condition the boy was. It was necessary to exclude her from the room, and the doctor remained, with Miss Sudie and Maj. Pagebrook. About midnight he stood and looked intently at the sick man's features, listening also to his hard-coming breath. He stood there full half an hour—then turning to Miss Sudie, he said :

"It's of no use, Miss Barksdale. Our young friend is beyond hope. He cannot live an hour. Perhaps you'd better inform his mother."

But before Miss Sudie could leave the bedside, Ewing roused himself for a moment, and tried to say something to her.

"Tell Robert—I got sick the very day—twenty-one—"

This was all Miss Sudie could hear, and she thought the patient's mind was wandering still, as it had been throughout his illness. And these incoherent words were the last the young man ever uttered.

About a week after Ewing's death Cousin Sarah Ann said to Maj. Pagebrook :

"Cousin Edwin, are you ever going to collect that money from Robert ? He promised to pay you on or before the fifteenth of November, and now it's nearly the last of the month and you haven't a line of explanation from him yet. I told you he wouldn't pay it till we made him. You oughtn't to've let him run away in your debt at all, and you wouldn't either, if you'd a'listened to me. Why don't you write to him ? "

" Well, I don't like to press the poor fellow. He's lost his money you know, and I reckon he finds it hard to pull through till January. He'll pay when he can, I reckon."

" O that's always the way with you! For my part I don't believe he had any money in the bank ; and besides he said there was some money coming to him on his salary, and he promised faithfully to pay you out of that. I told you he wouldn't, because I knew him. He tried to make out he was so much superior to the rest of us, and talked about 'reforming' poor Ewing, just as if the poor boy was a drunkard and—and—and—if you don't write I will, and I'll make him pay that money too, or I'll know why."

The conversation ended as such conversations usually did in Maj. Pagebrook's family, namely, by the abrupt departure of that gentleman from the house.

Cousin Sarah Ann evidently meant what she said, and her husband was no sooner out of the house than she got out her desk and wrote ; not to Robert, however, but to

Messrs. Steel, Flint & Sharp, attorneys and counselors at law, in New York city. Her note was not a long one, but it told the whole story of Robert's indebtedness from a not very favorable point of view, and closed with a request that the attorneys should "push the case by every means the law allows." This note was signed not with Cousin Sarah Ann's own but with her husband's name, and her first proceeding, after sealing the letter, was to send it by a servant to the post-office. She then ordered her carriage and drove over to Shirley.

.

## CHAPTER XX.

*Cousin Sarah Ann Takes Robert's Part.*

COUSIN SARAH ANN talked a good deal. Ill-natured people sometimes said she talked a good deal of nonsense, and possibly she did, but she never talked without a purpose, and she commonly managed to talk pretty successfully, too, so far as the accomplishment of her ends was concerned. In the present case, while I am wholly unprepared to say exactly why she wanted to talk, I am convinced that this excellent lady's visit to Shirley was undertaken solely for the purpose of securing an opportunity to talk.

Arrived there, she greeted her friends with her black-bordered handkerchief over her eyes, and for a time seemed hardly able to speak at all, so overpowering was her emotion. Then she said :

" I wouldn't think of visiting at such a time as this, of course, but Shirley seems so much like home, and I felt like I must have somebody to talk to who could sympathize with me. Dear Sudie was *so* good to me during— during it all."

After a time Cousin Sarah Ann composed herself, and

controlled her emotion sufficiently to converse connect-
edly without making painful pauses, though her voice
continued from first to last to be uncomfortably suggest-
ive of recent weeping.

"Have you had any news of Robert lately?" she
asked; "I do hope he's doing well."

"We've had no letters since Sudie's came while she
was at your house," said Colonel Barksdale. "He was
doing very well then, I believe, though he thought there
was no hope of recovering anything from the bank."

"I'm *so* sorry," said Cousin Sarah Ann, "for I love
Robert. He was so like an older brother to my poor boy.
I feel just like a mother to him, and I can't bear to have
anybody say anything against him."

"Nobody ever does say anything to his discredit, I
suppose," said Col. Barksdale. "He is really one of the
finest young men I ever knew, and the very soul of
honor, too. He comes honestly by that, however, for
his father was just so before him."

"That's just what I tell Cousin Edwin," said Cousin
Sarah Ann. "I tell him dear Robert means to do right,
and will do it just as soon as ever he can. Poor fellow!
he has been *so* unfortunate. Somebody must have made
Cousin Edwin suspicious of him, else he wouldn't think
so badly of poor Robert."

"Why, Sarah Ann, what do you mean?" asked Col.
Barksdale. "Surely Edwin has no reason to think ill of
Robert."

"No, that he hasn't; and that's what I tell him.
But he's been prejudiced and won't hear a word. He

says nothing about it to anybody but me, but he really suspects Robert of meaning to cheat him, and—"

"Cheat him!" cried all in a breath, "Why, how can that be ?"

"O it *can't* be, and so I tell Cousin Edwin ; but he insists that Robert told him he would pay that three hundred dollars on or before the fifteenth, and I reckon the poor boy hasn't been able to do it, or he would."

"Why, Sarah Ann, you don't tell me that Robert has failed to pay Edwin that money !" said the Colonel.

"Why, I thought you knew that, or I wouldn't have told you about it. No, he hasn't sent it yet ; but he will, of course, if I can keep Cousin Edwin from writing him violent letters about it."

"Hasn't he written to explain the delay ?" asked the Colonel.

"No ; and that's what Cousin Edwin always reminds me of when I try to take Robert's part. He says if he meant to be honest he would have written. I tell him I know how it is. I can fully understand Robert's silence. He has failed to get money when he expected it, I reckon, and has naturally hated to write till he could send the money. Poor boy ! I'm afraid he'll overwork himself and half starve himself, too, trying to get that money together, when we could wait for it just as well as not."

"There certainly can be no apology for his failure to write, after promising payment on a definite day," said Col. Barksdale ; "and I am both surprised and grieved that he should have acted in so unworthy a way !"

With this the Colonel arose and paced the room in evident anger. Robert's champion, Cousin Sarah Ann, could not stand this.

"Surely *you* are not going to turn against poor Robert without giving him a hearing, are you, Cousin Carter? I thought you too just for that, though I should never have mentioned the subject at all if I hadn't thought you all knew about it, and would take Robert's part like me."

"I shall give him a hearing," said the Colonel; "but in the meantime I must say his conduct has been very singular—very singular indeed."

"O he's only thoughtless!" said the excellent woman, in her anxiety to shield "dear Robert."

"No; he is not thoughtless. He never is thoughtless, whatever else he may be. If you wish to defend him, Sarah Ann, you must find some other excuse for his conduct. Confound the fellow! I can't help loving him, but if he isn't what I took him for, I'll—— "

The Colonel did not finish his threat; perhaps he hardly knew how.

"Now, Cousin Carter, please don't you fly into a passion like Cousin Edwin does," said Cousin Sarah Ann, pleadingly, "but wait till you find out all the facts. Write to Robert, and I'm sure he will explain it all. I wish I hadn't said a word about it."

"You did perfectly right, perfectly," said Colonel Barksdale. "If Robert has failed in a point of honor, I ought to know it, because in that case I have a duty to do—a painful one, but a duty nevertheless."

"O you men have no charity at all. You're *so* hard on one another, and I'm so sorry I said anything about it. Good-by, Cousin Mary. Good-by, Sudie dear. Come and see me, won't you? I miss you *so* much in my trouble. Come often. Come and stay some with me. Do. That's a dear."

And so Cousin Sarah Ann drove away, rejoicing in the consciousness that she had vigorously defended the absent Robert ; and perhaps rejoicing too in the conviction that that gentleman could not possibly explain his conduct to the satisfaction of Colonel Barksdale.

# CHAPTER XXI.

### *Miss Barksdale Expresses some Opinions.*

MISS SUDIE BARKSDALE was a very brave little woman, and she needed all her courage on the present occasion. She felt the absolute necessity there was that she should sit out Cousin Sarah Ann's conversation, and she sat it out, in what agony it is not hard to imagine. When that lady drove away Miss Sudie ran off to her room, where she remained for two or three hours. Upon her privacy we will not intrude.

Col. Barksdale called Billy from his office, and giving him the newly discovered facts, asked his opinion. Billy was simply thunderstruck.

"I can't understand it," said he; "Bob certainly had that money coming to him from his last year's salary, for he told me about it the day we first met in Philadelphia. If Bob isn't a man of honor, in the strictest sense of the term, I never was so deceived in anybody in my life. And yet this business looks as ugly as home-made sin. Bob knew perfectly well that if you or I had been at home when he left we wouldn't have allowed his protested draft to stand over at all, but would have paid it on the spot. He knew too that if he couldn't pay when he promised he could have written to me or to you explaining the matter, and we would have lent him the money for twenty years if necessary. I don't understand it at all. It looks ugly. It looks as if he meant to make that money clear."

"Well, my son," said Col. Barksdale, "I'll give him one chance to explain at any rate. I'll write to him immediately."

Accordingly the old gentleman went to his library and was engaged for some time in writing. After awhile there came a knock at his door, and Miss Sudie entered.

"Come in, daughter," said he, tenderly. "I want to talk with you."

"I thought you would," said the sad-eyed little maiden, "and that's why I came. I wanted our talk to be private."

"You're a good girl, my child." Then, after a pause, "This is bad news about Robert."

"Yes; and from a bad source," said Sudie.

"I do not understand you, daughter."

"We have the best of authority, Uncle Carter, for saying that 'men do not gather grapes of thorns!'"

"But, my child, I suppose there can be no doubt of the facts in this case, so far as we have them. We know the circumstances of Robert's indebtedness to Edwin, and whatever her motives may have been, Sarah Ann would hardly venture to say that he has neither paid nor written in explanation of his failure to do so, if he had done either."

" Perhaps not."

" Robert ought to have paid at any cost to himself if it were possible ; and if it were not, then he should have written in a frank, manly way, explaining his inability to fulfill his promise. Appearances are so strongly against him that I have written with very little hope of eliciting any satisfactory reply."

" Will you mind letting me see what you have written, Uncle Carter ?"

" No ; you may read the letter. Here it is."

Miss Sudie read it. It ran thus :

" I have just now learned that you have wholly failed to fulfill your solemn and deliberate promise, made on the eve of your departure from Shirley, to the effect that you would, without fail, take up your protested draft for three hundred dollars ($300), held by your Cousin Major Edwin Pagebrook, on or before the fifteenth (15th), day of this current month. It is now the thirtieth (30th), and hence your promise is fifteen (15) days over due. I learn also that you have failed to write in explanation of your delinquency or in any way to account or apologise for it. Permit me to say that as your conduct presents itself to me at this time, it is unworthy the gentleman which you profess to be, and I now demand of you either that you shall give me immediately a satisfactory explanation of the matter—and that, I must confess, sir, seems hardly possible—or that you shall at once write to my niece and adopted daughter, releasing her from her engagement with you."

Having finished reading the letter Sudie handed it back

to her uncle without a word of comment. Not that she was in this or in any other case afraid to express her opinion. Her uncle knew very well when he gave her the letter that she would say absolutely nothing about it until he should ask her, and he knew equally well that upon asking her he would get a perfectly honest expression of her thought, whatever it might happen to be. But Colonel Barksdale was, for the time, afraid to ask her opinion. He was a brave man and an honest one. He was known throughout the state as a lawyer of great ability and as a gentleman of the most undoubted sort. And yet at this moment he found himself afraid of a young girl, who stood in the relation of daughter to him —a girl who was never violent in word or act, a girl who honored him as a father and loved him with all her heart. He knew she would unhesitatingly speak the truth, and it was the truth of which he was afraid. He had not been aware, when he wrote, of any disposition to do Robert injustice, else, being a just man, he would have spurned the thought from him; but now that he felt bound to ask Miss Sudie for her opinion of his course, he became uncomfortably conscious that there had been other impulses than just ones governing him in his choice of language. At last he asked the dreaded question.

"What do you think, daughter?"

"I think you have not done yourself justice, Uncle Carter, in writing such a letter as that. The letter is not like you, at all."

"Well?"

" Do you mean why and wherefore ? "

" Yes.   Why and wherefore, Sudie ? "

" Because it is not like you to do an act of injustice, and when you are betrayed into one you misrepresent yourself."

" But wherein is my letter an act of injustice, my child ? "

" It assumes unproved guilt ; and I believe even criminals are entitled to a more favorable starting-point than that in their efforts to clear themselves."

" But, Sudie, I have not assumed that Robert is guilty. I have asked him to explain."

" Yes ; and in the very act of asking him to explain to you, his judge, you have assured him from the bench that the court believes an explanation impossible."

" Have I ?   Let me see."

After looking at the letter again he resumed :

" I believe you are right about that ; I will rewrite the letter, omitting the objectionable clause.   Is that all Sudie ? "

" Perhaps when you come to rewrite the letter you will see that its tone is as unjust as any words could possibly be.   It seems so to me."

" Let me try my hand again, daughter.   Keep your seat please while I write a new letter instead of rewriting the old one."

" There.   How will that do ? " he asked, as he handed the young woman this hastily-written note.

" MY DEAR ROBERT : We have just been hearing some news of you, which I trust you will be able to

contradict or explain. It is that you have failed to keep
your promise in the matter of your indebtedness to Major
Pagebrook, and that you have not even offered a word
by way of apology or explanation. The peculiar relations
in which you now stand to my family justify me, I think,
in asking you to explain a matter which, unexplained,
must reflect upon your character as an honorable man.
Please write to me by return mail."

"That is more like you, Uncle Carter. But I am
sorry to find that you are convinced, in advance, of Robert's guilt. You propose to sit in judgment upon his
case, and a court should not only appear but be free
from bias."

"Why, my daughter, I can hardly see how there can
be any possible excuse in a case like this. You cannot
deny that both facts and appearances are against him."

"I doubt whether we have the facts yet, Uncle Carter.
Aside from my knowledge of Cous— of Sarah Ann Pagebrook's general character, I saw her do a dishonorable
thing once. I saw her open and read a letter which was
not addressed to her, and I have no faith whatever in
her, or in any statement which comes from her or
through her."

Colonel Barksdale was probably not sorry that the conversation was interrupted at this point by the entrance of
a servant announcing a client. He felt that it would be
idle to argue with Sudie in a matter in which her feelings
were strongly enlisted, and he felt that in calling Robert
to an account he was doing a simple duty. He was, therefore, rather pleased than otherwise to have an accident

terminate a conversation which did not promise to terminate itself agreeably.

Miss Sudie went to her room and wrote to Robert on her own account. I am not at liberty to print her letter here, as I should greatly like to do, but the reader will readily guess its general nature. She told Robert in detail everything that had been said concerning him that day. She told him of her uncle's anger, and of the probability that everybody would believe him guilty if he failed to establish his innocence; but she assured him that she, at least, had no idea of doubting him for a moment.

"For your sake," she wrote, "I hope you will be able to offer a convincing explanation; but whether you can do that or not, Robert, *I know* that you are true and manly, and not even facts shall ever make me doubt your truth. I may never be able to see how your action has been right, but I shall know, nevertheless, that it has been so. My woman love is truer, to me at least, than logic—truer than fact—truer than truth itself."

All this was very illogical—very unreasonable, but very natural. It was "just like a woman" to set her emotions up in a holy place and compel her reason to do homage to them as to a god. And that is the very best thing there is about women, too. You and I, sir, would fare badly if in naming a woman wife we could not feel assured that her love will ever override her reason in matters concerning us.

## CHAPTER XXII.

### *Mr. Sharp Does His Duty.*

THE law firm of Steel, Flint & Sharp was a thoroughly well constituted one. Its organization was an admirable example of means perfectly adapted to the accomplishment of ends. It was not an eminent firm but it was an eminently successful one, particularly in the lines of business to which it gave special attention, and the leading one of these was collecting doubtful debts, as Cousin Sarah Ann had learned from one of the firm's cards which had fallen in her way. Indeed it was the accidental possession of this card which enabled her to put the matter of Robert's indebtedness into the hands of New York attorneys, and I suspect that she would never have thought of doing so at all but for the enticing words, fairly printed upon the card—"particular attention given to the collection of doubtful debts, due to non-residents of New York."

A prophet, we know, is not without honor save in his own country, and so it is not strange that the people who familiarly knew the countenances of the gentlemen

composing the firm of Steel, Flint & Sharp, esteemed
these gentlemen less highly than did those other people,
resident outside of New York, who could know these
counselors at law only through their profusely distributed cards and circulars. Such was the fact ; and as a
result it happened that the clients of the firm were
chiefly people who, living in other parts of the country,
were compelled to intrust their business in New York to
the hands of whatever attorneys they believed were the
leading ones in the metropolis. And it was to let people
know who were the leading lawyers of the city, that
Messrs. Steel, Flint & Sharp industriously scattered their
cards and circulars throughout the country.

Who Mr. Steel was I do not know, and I am strongly
inclined to suspect that the rest of the world, including
his partners, were in a state of equal ignorance. He was
never seen about the firm's offices, and never represented
anybody in court, but he was frequently referred to by
his partners, especially when clients were disposed to
complain of apparently exorbitant charges.

"Mr. Steel can not give his attention to a case, sir,
for nothing. His reputation is at stake, sir, in all we
undertake. I really do not feel at liberty to ask Mr.
Steel to authorize any reduction in this case, sir. He
gave his personal attention to the papers—his personal
attention, sir."

And this would commonly send clients away suppressed, if not satisfied.

Mr. Flint was well enough known. He managed the
business of the firm. It was he who always knew pre-

cisely what Mr. Steel's opinion was. He alone, of all the world, was able to speak positively of matters concerning Mr. Steel. Mr. Sharp was his junior in the firm, though considerably his senior in years. For Mr. Sharp Mr. Flint entertained not one particle of respect, because that gentleman was not always what his name implied. Mr. Sharp left to himself would have been hopelessly honest and straightforward. He would have gone to the dogs, speedily, Mr. Flint said, but for his association with himself.

"But you have excellent ability in your way, Sharp, excellent ability," he would say when in a good humor. "You are a capital executive officer—a very good lieutenant. Your ideas of what to do in any given case are not always good, but when I tell you what to do you do it, Sharp. I always know you will do what I tell you, and do it well too."

Mr. Sharp usually came to the office an hour earlier than Mr. Flint did, in order that he might have everything ready for Mr. Flint's examination when that gentleman should arrive. He read the letters, drew up papers, and was prepared to give his partner in each case the facts upon which his opinion or advice was necessary.

On the morning of December 3d, Mr. Flint came softly into his office and, after hanging up his overcoat and warming his hands at the register, went into his inner den, saying, as he sat down :

"I'm ready for you now, Sharp."

Mr. Sharp arose from his desk and entered the private room, with his hands full of papers.

" What's the first thing on docket, Sharp ? "

" Well, here's a collection to be made. Debtor, Robert Pagebrook, temporarily in the city. Boarding place not known. Writes for the newspapers, so I can easily find him. Creditor Edwin Pagebrook, of——— Court House, Virginia. Debtor got creditor to cash draft for three hundred dollars. Draft protested. Debtor came away, and promised to take up paper by fifteenth November. Hasn't done it. Instructions 'push him.' "

"Any limitations ? "

" No."

" What have you done ? "

" Nothing yet ; I'll look him up to-day and dun him."

" Yes, and let him get away from you. Sharp do you know that Julius Cæsar is dead ? "

" Certainly."

" I'm glad to hear that you do know something then. Don't you see the point in this case ? Go and make out affidavits on information. This fellow Robert what's his name is a 'transient,' and we'll get an order of arrest all ready and then you can dun him with some sense. Have your officer with you or convenient, and if he don't pay up, chuck him in jail. That's the way to do it. Never waste time dunning 'transients' when there's a ghost of a chance to cage them."

" Well, but there don't seem to be any fraud here. The man seems to have had funds in the bank, only the bank suspended."

" Sharp, you'll learn a little law after awhile, I hope. Don't you know the courts never look very sharply after cases where transients are concerned ? How do we know he had money in the bank ? Is there anything to show it ?"

" No; I believe not."

" Well, then, don't you go to making facts in the interest of the other side. Let him make that out if he can. You just draw your affidavits to suit our purposes, not his. Go on to state that he drew a certain bill of exchange, and represented that he had funds, and so fraudulently obtained money, and all that ; and then go on to say that his draft upon presentation was protested, and that instead of making it good he absconded. Be sure to say absconded, Sharp, it's half the battle. Courts haven't much use for men that abscond and then turn up in New York. Make your case strong enough, though. We only swear on information, you know, so if we do put it a little strong it don't matter. There. Go and fix it up right away, and then catch your man."

A few hours later, as Robert Pagebrook sat writing in his room, Mr. Sharp and another man were shown in. Mr. Sharp opened the conversation.

" This is Mr. Pagebrook, I believe ?"

" Yes, sir."

" Mr. *Robert* Pagebrook ?"

" Yes. That is my name."

" Thank you. My name is Sharp, of the firm of Steel, Flint & Sharp. That's our card, sir. I have called to solicit the payment, sir, of a small amount due Mr. Edwin Pagebrook, who has written asking us to collect it for him. The amount is three hundred dollars, I

"LET HIM SERVE IT AT ONCE, THEN."

think. Yes. Here is the draft. Can you let me have the money to-day, Mr. Pagebrook?"

"I have already remitted one third the amount, sir," said Robert, "and I hope to send the remainder in installments very soon. At present it is simply impossible for me to pay anything more."

"Have you a receipt for the amount remitted?" asked the lawyer.

"No. It was sent only yesterday. But if you will hold the draft a week or ten days longer, I will be able, within that time, to earn the whole of the amount remaining due, and your client will advise you, I am sure, of the receipt of the hundred dollars already sent."

"We are not authorised to wait, sir," said Mr. Sharp. "On the contrary our instructions are positive to push the case."

"But what can I do?" asked Robert. "I have already sent every dollar I had, and until I earn more I can pay no more."

"The case is a peculiar one, sir. It has the appearance of a fraudulent debt and an attempt to run away from it. I must do my duty by my client, sir; and so this gentleman, who is a sheriff's officer, has an order for your arrest, which I must ask him to serve if you do not pay the debt to day."

"Let him serve it at once, then," said Robert. "I can not pay now."

# CHAPTER XXIII.

## *Mr. Pagebrook Takes a Lesson in the Law.*

AS Robert was unable to give bail without calling upon his friend Dudley, which he determined not to do in any case, he was taken to the jail and locked up. Upon his arrival there he employed a messenger to carry a note to a young lawyer with whom he happened to be slightly acquainted, asking him to come to the jail at once.   When he arrived Robert said to him :

"Let me tell you in the outset, Mr. Dyker, that I have no money and no friends ; wherefore if you allow me to consult you at all, it must be with the understanding that I cannot possibly pay you for your services until I can make the money.   If you are willing to trust me to that extent, we can proceed to business."

"You are very honorable, sir, to inform me, before-hand, of this fact.   Pray go on.   I will do what I can for you."

"In the first place, then," said Robert, "I am a little puzzled to know how or why I am locked up.   You have the papers, will you tell me how it is ?"

"O it's plain enough. You are held under an order of arrest."

"But I don't understand. I thought imprisonment for debt was a thing of the past, in this country at least, and my only offense is indebtedness. Is it possible that men may still be imprisoned for debt in America?"

"Well, that is about it," said the lawyer. "We have abolished the name but retain the thing in a slightly modified form—in New York at least. Theoretically you are not imprisoned, but merely held to answer. The plaintiffs have made out a case of fraud and non-residence, and so they had plain sailing."

"But I always understood that our constitution or our law or something else secured every man against imprisonment except by due process of law, and gave to every accused person the right to be confronted with his accusers, to cross-examine witnesses, and to have his guilt or innocence passed upon by a jury of his countrymen."

"That is the theory; but there are some classes of cases which are practically exceptions, and yours is one of them."

"Then," said Robert, "it is true, is it, that an American may be arrested and sent to jail without trial, upon the mere strength of affidavits made by lawyers who know nothing of the facts except what they have heard from distant, irresponsible, and personally interested clients—affidavits upon information, I believe you call them?"

"Well, you put it a little strongly, perhaps, but those are the facts in New York. Respectable lawyers, however, are careful to satisfy themselves of the facts before proceeding at all in such cases; and so the law, which is a very convenient one, rarely ever works injustice, I think —not once in twenty times, I should say."

"But," said Robert, "the personal liberty of every non-resident and some resident debtors is, or in some cases may be, dependent solely upon the character of attorneys, as I understand you."

"In some cases, yes. But pardon me. Had we not better come to the matter in hand?"

"As we are not a legislature perhaps it would be better," said Robert. He then proceeded to relate the facts of the case, beginning with his drawing of the draft in good faith, its protest, and his consequent perplexity.

"I did not 'abscond' at all," he continued, "but came away to see if I could save something from the wreck of the bank, and to seek work. In leaving, I promised to pay the debt on or before the fifteenth of last month, feeling certain that I could do so. I failed to do it, through —— never mind, I failed to do it, but I have been trying hard ever since to get the money and discharge the obligation. I yesterday remitted a hundred dollars, and should have sent the rest as fast as I could make it. These are the facts. Now how am I to get out of here?"

"You have nobody to go your bail?"

"Nobody."

"And no money?"

"None. I sold my watch in order to get money on which to live while I was looking for work."

"You did have money enough to your credit in that bank to have made your draft good if the bank hadn't suspended?"

"Yes."

"You can swear to that?"

"Certainly."

"Then I think we can manage this matter without much difficulty. We can admit the facts but deny the fraudulent intent, in affidavits of our own, and get discharged on that ground. I think we can easily overthrow the theory of fraud by showing that you actually had the money in bank and swearing that you drew against it in good faith."

"Pardon me; but in doing that I should be bound, should I not, in honor if not in law, to state all the facts of the case in my affidavit? The theory of the proceeding is that I am putting the court in possession of all the facts and withholding nothing, is it not?"

"Well—yes. I suppose it is."

"Then let us abandon that plan forthwith."

"But my dear sir——"

"Pray don't argue the point. My mind is fully made up. Is there no other mode of securing my release?"

"Yes; you might schedule out under article 5 of the Non-Imprisonment Act, I think."

"How is that?"

"It is a sort of insolvency or bankruptcy proceeding, by which you come into court—any court of record—and offer to give up everything you have to your creditors, giving a sworn catalogue of all your debts and all your property, and praying release on the ground that you are unable to do more."

"Well, as I have literally nothing in the way of property just now, that mode of procedure seems to fit my case precisely," said Robert, whose courage and good humor and indomitable cheerfulness stood him in good stead in this time of very sore trial. The world looked gloomy enough to him then in whatever way he chose to look at it, but the instinct of fight was large within him, and in the absence of other joys he felt a savage pleasure in knowing that his life henceforth must be a constant struggle against fearful odds—odds of prejudice as well as of poverty; for who could now take him by the hand and say to others this is my friend?

"It's too late to accomplish anything to-day, Mr. Pagebrook," said the lawyer, looking at his watch; "but I will be here by ten o'clock to-morrow morning, and we will then go to work for your deliverance, which we can effect, I think, pretty quick. Good evening, sir."

# CHAPTER XXIV.

*Mr. Pagebrook Cuts himself loose from the Past and Plans a Future.*

WHEN the lawyer had gone Robert sat down to deliberate upon the situation and to decide what was to be done in matters aside from the question of his release. He had that morning received Col. Barksdale's letter and Miss Sudie's. These must be answered at once, and he was not quite certain how he should answer them. After turning the matter over he determined upon his course and, according to his custom, having determined what to do he at once set about doing it. Having brought a supply of paper and envelopes from his room he had only to borrow pen and ink from the attendant.

His first letter was addressed to the president of the college from which he had received his appointment as professor, and it consisted of a simple resignation, with no explanation except that contained in the sentence :

"I can ill afford to surrender the position or the salary, but there are painful circumstances surrounding me, which compel me to this course. Pray excuse me from a fuller statement of the case."

To Col. Barksdale he wrote :

"Your letter surprises me only in its kindness and

gentleness of tone.    Under the circumstances I could have forgiven a good deal of harshness.  For your forbearance, however, you have my hearty thanks.    And now as to the subject matter of your note: I am sorry to say I can offer neither denial nor satisfactory explanation of the facts alleged against me.    I must bear the blame that attaches to what I have done, and bearing that blame I know my duty to you and your family.    I shall write by this mail to Miss Barksdale volunteering a release, which otherwise you would have a right to demand of me."

Sealing this and directing it, Robert came to the hardest task of all—the writing of a letter to Cousin Sudie.

"I hardly know how to write to you," he wrote. "Your generous faith in me in spite of everything is more than I had any right to expect, and more, I think, than you have any right, in justice to yourself, to give me.    I thank you for it right heartily, but I feel that I must not accept it.    When you listened to my words of love and gave them a place in your heart, I was a gentleman without reproach.    Now a stain is upon my name, which I can never remove.    The man to whom you promised your hand was not the absconding debtor who writes you this from a jail.    I send this letter, therefore, to offer you a release from your engagement with me, if indeed any release be necessary.    You cannot afford to know me or even to remember me hereafter.    Forget me, then, or, if you cannot wholly forget, remember me only as an adventurer, who for a paltry sum sold his good name.

"Good-by.    I wish you well with all my heart."

As he sealed these letters Robert felt that his hopes for

the future were sealed up with them, and that the post
which should bear them away would carry with it the
better part of his life. And yet he did not wholly surrender himself to despair, as a weaker man might have done.
The old life was gone from him forever. The only people whom he had known as in any sense his own would
grasp his hand no more, and if they ever thought of him
again it would be only to regret that they had known him
at all. All this he felt keenly, but it did not follow that
he should abandon himself, as a consequence. He was
still a young man, and there was time enough for him to
make a new life for himself—to find new friends and to
do some worthy work in the world; and to the planning
of this new life he at once addressed himself.

He would teach no longer, and now that he had cut
himself loose from that profession there was opportunity
to do something at the business which he had found so
agreeable of late. He would devote himself hereafter
wholly to writing, and at the first opportunity he would
become a regular member of the staff of some paper.
Even if his earnings with his pen should prove small,
what did that matter? He could never think of marry-
ing now, and a very little would suffice to supply all his
wants, his habits of life being simple and regular. It
stung him when he remembered that there was a stain
upon his name which could never be removed; but that,
he knew, he must bear, and so he resolved to bear it
bravely, as it becomes a man to bear all his burdens.

With thoughts like these the stalwart young fellow
sank to sleep on the bed assigned him in the jail.

## CHAPTER XXV.

*In which Miss Sudie Acts very Unreasonably.*

THE men who make up mails and handle great bags full of letters every day of their lives grow accustomed to the business, I suppose, and learn after awhile to regard the bags and their contents merely as so many pounds of "mail matter." Otherwise they would soon become unfit for their duties. If they could weigh those bags with other than material scales—if they could know how many human hopes and fears; how much of human purpose and human despair; how many joys and how much of wretchedness those bags contain; if they could hear the moans that utter themselves inside the canvas; if they could know the varying purposes with which all those letters have been written, and the various effects they are destined to produce; if our mail carriers could know and feel all these things, or the half of them, we should shortly have no mail carriers at all. But fortunately there are prosaic souls enough in the world to make all necessary mail agents and postmasters, and undertakers and grave-diggers out of.

In the small mail bag thrown off at the Court House one December morning, there was one little package of

New York letters—three letters in all, but on those three letters hung the happiness of several human lives. Of one of them we shall learn nothing for the present. The other two, from Robert Pagebrook to his uncle and Miss Barksdale, we have already been permitted to read. When these were received at Shirley, Miss Sudie took hers to her own room and read it there, after which she sat down and answered it. Col. Barksdale read his with no surprise, as he had not been able to imagine any possible explanation of Robert's conduct; and now that that gentleman frankly confessed that there was none, he accepted the confession as a bit of evidence in the case, for which he had waited merely as a matter of form. It was his duty now to talk again with his niece, but he was very tender always in his dealings with her, and felt an especial tenderness now that she must be suffering sorely. He quietly inquired where she was, and learning that she was in her own room, he refrained from summoning her himself, and gave her maid particular instructions to allow no one else to intrude upon her privacy upon any pretense whatsoever.

"Lucy," he said, to the colored woman, "your Miss Sudie wishes to be alone for awhile. Sit down in the passage near her door, but don't knock, and don't allow any one else to knock. When she wishes to see any one she will open the door herself, and until then I do not want her disturbed."

Then going into the dining-room, where Dick was polishing the mahogany with a large piece of cork, he said:

"Dick, go out to the office and ask your Mas' Billy if

he will be good enough to come to me in the library. I want to talk with him."

When Billy came in his father showed him Robert's letter.

"The thing looks very ugly," said the younger gentleman.

"Very ugly, indeed," said his father; "but the confounded rascal holds up his head under it all, and acts as honorably in Sudie's case as if he had never acted otherwise than as a gentleman should. He is a puzzle to me. But, of course, this must end the matter. We can have nothing whatever to do with him hereafter."

"But how is it, father, that they have managed to imprison him?"

"I presume they have secured an order of arrest under that New York statute which seems to have been devised as a means of securing to creditors all the advantages of imprisonment for debt without shocking the better sense of the community, which is clearly against such imprisonment. The majority of people rarely ever pay any attention to the fact so long as they are spared the name of odious things. No debtors' prison would be allowed to stand in the United States, of course, but the common jails answer all purposes when a way for getting debtors locked up in them has been devised."

"But how does it happen, father," asked Mr. Billy, "that only New York has such a statute?"

"Well, in New York the commercial interest overrides every other, and commercial men naturally attach undue importance to the collection of debts, and look with

favor upon everything which tends to facilitate it. These
things always reflect the feeling rather than the opinion
of a community. In new countries, where horses are of
more importance than anything else, horse-stealing is
pretty sure to be punished with death, either by law or
by the mob, which is only public sentiment embodied.
Here in Virginia you know how impossible it is to get
anything like an effective statute for the suppression of
dueling, simply because the ultimate public sentiment
practically approves of personal warfare. But, I confess,
I did not know that the New York statute could be
stretched to cover a case like Robert's. As I understand
it, there must be some evidence of fraud in the inception
of the transaction."

"They proceed upon affidavits, I believe," said Billy,
"and when that is done it isn't hard to make out a case,
if the attorney is unscrupulous enough."

"That's true. But isn't it curious that Edwin should
have proceeded so promptly to harsh measures? He is
so mild of temper that this surprises me."

"Cousin Edwin doesn't always act out his own character, you know, father. His wife is the stronger willed
of the two."

"True. I hadn't thought of that. However, it serves
the young rascal right."

At this point of the conversation Cousin Sudie's knock
was heard at the inner door, and Col. Barksdale opening
the outer one said :

"You'd better go out this door, William. It would
embarrass Sue to find you here just now."

"Come in my daughter," he said, admitting Miss Sudie. "Sit down. I am greatly pained, on his account as well as yours, to find that Robert has no explanation to offer. But, of course, this ends it all, and you must take a little trip somewhere, my dear, until you forget all about it. Where shall we go?"

"I do not care to go anywhere, Uncle Carter," replied the little maiden, without the faintest echo of a sob in her voice. "I am sorry for poor Robert, but not because I think him guilty of any dishonorable action, for indeed I do not."

"But, my dear, it will never do——"

"Pray hear me out, Uncle Carter, and then I will listen to anything you have to say. I love you as a father, as you know perfectly well. Indeed I have never known you as anything else. I have always obeyed you unquestioningly, and I shall not begin to disobey you now. I shall do precisely what you tell me to do, *so long as I remain in your house.*"

"What do you mean by that, daughter?" asked her uncle, startled by the singular emphasis which Miss Sudie gave to the last clause of the sentence.

"Merely this, Uncle Carter. I cannot consent to do that which my conscience teaches me is a crime, even at your command; but while I remain at Shirley as a daughter of the house I must obey as a daughter. If you command me to do anything which I cannot do without sinning against my conscience, then I must not obey you, and when I can't obey you I must cease to be your daughter. I shall conceal nothing from you, Uncle

Carter ; you know that, and I beg of you don't command me to do the things which I must not do. I love you and it would kill me—no, it would not do that, but it would pain me more than I can possibly say, to leave Shirley."

Col. Barksdale leaned his head sorrowfully upon his hand. He loved this girl and held her as his own. Moreover, he had solemnly promised his dying brother to care for her always as a father cares for his children, and an oath could not have been more sacred in his eyes than this promise was. Without raising his head he asked :

"You mean, Sudie, that you will not accept Robert's release ?"

"Yes, uncle, that is what I mean." This was sorrowfully and gently said, but firmly too.

"He has offered to release you ; has he not ?"

"Yes."

"And in so offering, did he express or hint a wish that you should not accept his release ?"

"No. On the contrary he assumed that I would accept it, and that I must do so in justice to myself. Here is his letter. Read it if you please."

Col. Barksdale read the letter, with which the reader is already familiar, and, handing it back, said :

"A very proper and manly letter."

"Because it came from a very proper and manly man," said Miss Sudie.

"You don't believe he has been guilty of the dishonorable acts laid to his charge, then ?"

"Of the acts, yes. Of the dishonor, no," said the girl.

"On what ground do you base your persistent good opinion of him?"

"On my persistent faith in him."

"Your faith is very unreasonable, my dear."

"Perhaps so, but it exists nevertheless."

"Have you answered his letter?"

"Yes, sir; and I have brought my answer for you to read, if you care to do so," she said, taking her letter out of her desk, which lay in her lap, and giving it to her uncle, who read as follows:

"MY DEAR ROBERT:—I am not in the least surprised by your letter. I knew you would offer to release me from my engagement, because I knew you were a man of honor. I have never for a moment doubted that, and I do not doubt it now. Your character weighs more with me than any mere facts can. I know you are an honorable man, and knowing that I shall not let other people's doubts upon the subject govern my action. When I 'listened to your words of love, and gave them a place in my heart,' you were, as you say, 'a gentleman without reproach'; and the reproach which lies upon you now does not make you less a gentleman. It is an unjust reproach, and your manliness in bearing it and offering to accept its consequences, only serves to mark you still more distinctly as a gentleman. Shall I be less honorable, less fearlessly true than you? When I gave you my heart and promised you my hand, you had friends in abundance. Now that you have none, I have no idea of withdrawing either the gift or the promise.

"You say you can never clear your name of the stain

which is upon it now. For that I am heartily sorry, for your sake, but as I know that the stain does not rightly belong there it becomes my duty and my pleasure to bear it with you. I shall retain my faith in you and my love for you, and I shall profess them too on all proper occasions, and when you claim me as your wife I shall hold up Mrs. Robert Pagebrook's head as proudly as I now hold Susan Barksdale's.

"Under other circumstances I should have thought it unmaidenly to write in this way, but there must be no doubt of my meaning now. If you ever ask a release from your promise, with or without reason, I trust you know me well enough to know that it will be granted—but from my promise I shall ask none. Another reason for the frankness of this letter is that I want you, in your trouble, to know how implicitly I trust your honor; and I should certainly never trust such a letter in any but the cleanest of hands.

"Uncle Carter will see this before it goes, and he will know, as it is right that he should, that I have not availed myself of your proffered release. . . . . ."

The omitted sentences with which the letter closed are not for our eyes. Even Colonel Barksdale refused to read them, feeling that they were sacred, and that the permission given him to read the letter extended no further than the end of the sentence last set down in the extract above given.

Returning the sheet he said : "I suppose you have written this after giving the matter full consideration, daughter ?"

"I never act without knowing what I am doing, Uncle Carter."

"Well, my child, I think you are wrong, but I shall not ask you to do anything which your conscience condemns. I shall not ask you to withhold your letter, or to alter it, but I would prefer that you hold it until tomorrow, so that you may be quite sure you want to send it as it is. Will you mind doing that?"

"No, Uncle Carter. I will keep it till to-morrow, if you wish, but I shall not change my mind concerning it. You are very good to me. Thank you;" and kissing his forehead, she left him, not to return to her room as a more sentimental woman would have done, but to go about her daily duties, with a sober face, it is true, but with all her accustomed regularity and attention to business.

## CHAPTER XXVI.

*In which Miss Sudie Adopts the Socratic Method.*

WHEN Miss Sudie left him Col. Barksdale again sent for his son and told him of that young woman's unreasonable determination.

"I expected that, father, and am not at all surprised," said the young man.

"Why, my son? Had you talked the matter over with her?"

"No. But I know Sudie too well to expect her to give up her faith in Bob while he is under a cloud and in trouble too. She has a mighty good head on her shoulders; but what's a woman's head worth when her heart pulls the other way? She overrides her own reason as coolly as if it were worth just nothing at all, and puts everybody else's out of the way with the utmost indifference. I know her of old. She used to take my part that way whenever I got into a boyish scrape, and before she had done with it she always convinced me, along with everybody else, that I had done nothing to be ashamed of. The fact is, father, I like that in Sudie. She's the truest little woman I ever saw, and she sticks to her friends like mutton gravy to the roof of your mouth," said Billy, unable, even at such a time as this, to restrain his passion for strange metaphors.

"The trait is a noble one, certainly," said the old gentleman; "but for that very reason, if for no other, we must do what we can to keep her from sacrificing herself to a noble faith in an unworthy man. Don't you think so?"

"Without doubt. But what can we do? You say you do not feel free to control her."

"We can at least do our duty. I have talked with her, and now I want you to do the same. She will not shun the conversation, I think, for she is a brave girl."

"I will see what I can do, father," said the young man. "Possibly I may persuade her to let the matter rest where it is, for the present at least, and even that will be something gained."

Col. Barksdale was right in thinking that Miss Sudie would not seek to avoid a conversation with Billy. On the contrary she wished especially to say something to this young gentleman, and for that very purpose she sought him in the office. He and she had been brought up as brother and sister, and there was no feeling of restraint between them now that they were grown man and woman.

"Cousin Billy," she said, sitting down near him, "I want to talk with you about Robert. I want to remind you, if you will let me, of your duty to him."

"What do you conceive my duty to be in the case, Sudie?" asked Billy.

"To defend him," said Miss Sudie.

" But how can I do that, Sudie, in face of the facts ? "

" You believe then that Robert Pagebrook, whom you know thoroughly, has done the dishonorable things laid to his charge ? "

" Well," said Billy, feeling himself hardly prepared for this kind of attack, " I confess I should never have thought him capable of doing such things."

" Why would you never have thought him capable of doing them, Cousin Billy ? "

" O well, because he always seemed to be such an honorable fellow," said Billy.

" You did believe him honorable, then ? " asked this young female Socrates.

" Certainly ; you know that Sudie."

" On what did you base that belief, Cousin Billy ? "

" Why, on his way of doing things, on my knowledge of him, of course ; " replied Billy.

" Well, then, is that knowledge of him of no value now ? " asked Sudie.

" How do you mean ? "

" I mean does your knowledge of Robert weigh nothing now ? Are you ready to believe on imperfect evidence, that Robert Pagebrook, who you know was an honorable man, is not now an honorable man ? Doesn't his character weigh anything with you ? Do you believe his character has changed, or do you think it possible that he simulated that character and did it so perfectly as to deceive us all ? Doesn't it seem more probable that there is some mistake about this business ? In short, how can you believe Robert guilty of a thing which you know very well he wouldn't do for his head? If you 'wouldn't have believed it,' why do you believe it?"

Mr. Billy was stunned. He had been prepared for tears. He had expected to find in Sudie an unreasoning faith. He had looked for an obstinate determination on her part to adhere to her purpose. But for this kind of illogical logic he had made no preparation whatever. It had never entered his head that Miss Sudie would seriously undertake to argue the matter. The evidence against Robert he had accepted as unquestionable, and he had not expected Miss Sudie to question it in this way.

"But, Cousin Sudie, you overlook the fact that Robert has confessed the very thing which you say is unlikely."

"No; he has not confessed anything of the sort. Indeed he seems to have carefully avoided doing so. In his letter to Uncle Carter he merely says, 'I can offer neither denial nor explanation of the facts alleged against me.' To me he only says, 'a stain is upon my name.' He nowhere says, 'I am guilty.'"

"But, Sudie," said Billy, "if he a'n't guilty, why can't he offer either 'denial or explanation'?"

"That I do not know; but I don't find it half as hard to believe that there may be good reasons for that, as to believe that an honorable man—a man whom we both know to be an honorable one—has done a dishonorable thing."

"But, Sudie, why didn't Bob borrow the money of father or of me, if he honestly couldn't pay? He knew we would gladly lend it to him."

" I'm glad you mentioned that. If Robert had wanted to swindle anybody, how much easier it would have been for him to write to you or Uncle Carter, saying he couldn't pay and asking you to take up his protested draft for him. He knew you would have done it, and he could then have accomplished his purpose without any exposure. Almost any excuse would have satisfied you or Uncle Carter, and so the thing would have gone on for years. Wouldn't he have done exactly that, Cousin Billy, if he had wanted to swindle anybody? Men don't often covet a bad name for its own sake."

" Clearly, Sudie, I am getting the worst of this argument. You are a better sophist than I ever gave you credit for being. But it's hard to believe that black is white. I'll tell you what I'll do, though, Sudie. I'll do my very best to believe that there is some sort of faint possibility that facts a'n't facts, and hold myself, as nearly as I can, in readiness to believe that something may turn up in Bob's favor. If anything were to turn up I'd be as glad of it as anybody."

" But I'm not satisfied with that, Cousin Billy."

" What more do you ask, Sudie ?"

" That you shall hold yourself in readiness to help turn something up whenever an opportunity offers. Keep a sharp lookout for things which may possibly have a bearing upon this matter, and follow up any clue you may get. Won't you do that for my sake, Cousin Billy ?"

" I'd do anything for your sake, Sudie, and I'd give a hundred dollars for your faith."

And so ended the conversation. Mr. Billy, it must be

confessed, had done little toward the accomplishment of
the task he had set himself.   But as he himself put it :
" What on earth was a fellow to do with a faith which
made incontestable truths out of impossibilities, and
scattered facts before it like a flock of partridges ?"   Mr.
Billy fully appreciated the unreasonableness of Miss
Sudie's logic, and yet, in spite of all, he could not help
entertaining a sort of half hope that something would
occur to vindicate Robert—a hope born of nothing more
substantial than Miss Sudie's enthusiastic belief in her
lover.

# CHAPTER XXVII.

*Mr. Pagebrook Accepts an Invitation to Lunch and another Invitation.*

ON the morning after Robert's incarceration, his attorney came at the appointed hour for the purpose of preparing the papers on which application was to be made for his discharge.

"I have the affidavits all ready, I believe, Mr. Pagebrook, and we have only to make a complete list of your property."

"That will be easily done, sir," said Robert, with a feeling of grim amusement; "as I have literally nothing except my trunk and its contents."

"You have your claim on that bank for money deposited. I suppose that must be included, though it is only a *chose* in action."

"O put it in, by all means," said Robert. "I do not wish to misrepresent anything or to withhold anything. I only wish the *chose* in action, as you call it, were of sufficient value to discharge the debt. I should then quit here free from all indebtedness, except to you for your fee; and should not have this thing to pay.'

"Your discharge, I think, will free you, in law, from——"

"But it will not free me in honor sir. It will give me time, however; and the very first use I shall make of that time will be to earn the money with which to pay off this, my only debt. I should never ask a discharge at all if the asking supposed any purpose on my part to avoid the payment of the debt. Pardon me; this talk must sound odd to you, coming from a man in my present position. I forgot that I am an absconding debtor. You will think my talk a cheap kind of honesty, costing nothing."

"No, Pagebrook—if you will allow me to drop the 'Mister'—I should trust you in any transaction, though I have not known you a week. I don't believe you are an absconding debtor, and I'm not going to believe it on the strength of any oaths Messrs. Steel, Flint & Sharp may make." As he said this the young lawyer took Robert's hand, and Robert found himself wholly unable to utter a word by way of reply. He did not want to shed tears in the presence of his jail attendants, but the lawyer saw them standing in his eyes, and prevented any effort at replying by turning at once to the matter in hand.

"Come, Pagebrook," he said, "this isn't business. Let me see; what bank was it that you deposited with?"

"The Essex," said Robert.

"The Essex!" said the lawyer. "What was that I saw in the Tribune this morning about that bank? I think it was the Essex. Let me see;" running his eye over the columns of the newspaper, which he had taken from his pocket.

"Ah! here it is. By George! My dear Pagebrook, I

congratulate you. Your bank has resumed. See, here is the item :

"'PHILADELPHIA, DEC. 3D.—The Essex Bank, of this city, which suspended payment some weeks since, will resume business to-morrow. Its affairs were found to be in a very favorable condition, and at a meeting of the stockholders, held to-day, the deficit in its assets was covered, and its capital made good by subscription. It is not thought that any run will be made upon it, but ample preparations have been made to meet such a contingency.'

"Again I congratulate you, right heartily."

"This means then, that my sixteen hundred dollars—that was the total amount of my deposit—is intact, and that I may check against it as soon as I choose, does it ?"

"Certainly."

"Then let us suspend our preparations for securing my release. I will pay out of this instead of begging out. I will draw at once for enough to cover this debt and your fees, and ask you to put the draft into bank for collection. We will have returns by the day after to-morrow, doubtless, and I shall then go out of here with my head up."

"We'll end this business sooner than that, Pagebrook," said the lawyer. "Draw your draft, I'll indorse it, take it to the bank where I deposit, get it cashed at once, and have you out of here in time for a two o'clock lunch. You'll lunch with me, of course."

"Pardon me, but you have no means of knowing that I have any money in that bank," said Robert.

" Yes, indeed I have."

" What is it ?"

" Your word.   I told you I would trust you."

Robert looked at the man a moment, and then taking his hand, said :

" I accept your confidence frankly.   Thank you. Draw the draft, please, and I will sign it."

The draft was soon drawn, and at two o'clock that day —just twenty-four hours after his arrest—Robert sat down to lunch with his friend, in a down-town eating-house.

While the two gentlemen were engaged with their lunch, Robert's friend Dudley, who had been eating a chop at the farther end of the room, espied his acquaintance, and approaching him said :

" How are you, Pagebrook ?   Are you specially engaged for this afternoon ? "

" No, I believe not," said Robert.   " I have nothing to do except to finish an article which I want to offer you to-morrow, and I can do that to-night."

" Suppose you come up to the office, then, after you finish your lunch.   I want to talk with you."

" I will be there within half an hour, if that will suit you," said Robert.

" Very well ; I'll expect you."

Accordingly, Robert bade his friend adieu after lunch, and went immediately to the editor's room.

Mr. Dudley closed the door, first saying to his messenger, who sat in the anteroom ;

" I shall be busy for some time, Eddie, and can't see

anybody. If any one calls, tell him I am closeted with a gentleman on important business and can see nobody. Now, Pagebrook," he resumed, taking his seat, "you ought to quit teaching."

"Why?" asked Robert.

"Well, you're a born writer certainly, and if I am not greatly mistaken, a born journalist too. You have a knack of knowing just what points people want to hear about. I've been struck with that in every article you have written for me, and especially in this last one. Do you know I've rejected no less than a dozen well-written articles on that very subject, just because they treated every phase of it except the right one, and didn't come within a mile of that. Now you've hit it exactly, as you always do. You've got hold of precisely the things that nobody knows anything about and everybody wants to know all about, and that's journalism."

"Thank you," said Robert. "You really think, then, that I might make myself a successful journalist if I were to try?"

"I know you would. You have precisely the right sort of ideas. You discriminate between the things that are wanted and the things that are not. I have long since discovered that this thing that men call writing ability and journalistic ability isn't like anything else. It crops out where you would never look for it, and where you think it ought to be it isn't. You can't coax or nurse it into existence to save your life. If a man has it he has it, and if he hasn't it he hasn't it, and nobody can give it to him. It isn't contagious, and I honestly believe it isn't acquirable. And that's why I'm certain of you. You've shown that you have it, and one showing is as good as a hundred."

"I am greatly pleased," said Robert, "to know that you think so well of me in this respect, for I have resigned my professorship and determined to make my way, to the best of my ability, as a journalist, hereafter?"

"You have?"

"Yes; I sent my letter of resignation yesterday."

"I'm heartily glad of it, old fellow, and selfishly glad, too, for it was to persuade you to do that that I sat down to talk to you. You see my health is not very good lately; the fact is I have been using the spur too much, and am pretty well run down with overwork. The publishers have been urging me to get an assistant, and the trouble is to get one who can really relieve me of a share of the work. I can get plenty of people to undertake it, but I have to go over their work to be sure of it, and it's easier to do it myself from the first. Now you are just the man I want, if you can stand the salary. The publishers will let me pay forty dollars a week. You can make more than that from the outside, I suppose, but it's better to be in a regular situation, I think. How would you like to try the thing?"

"Nothing could be more to my taste. I think I should like this better than daily paper work, and besides it gives one a better opportunity for growth. But before we talk any more about it I feel myself in honor bound to tell you what has happened to me lately. If you care then to repeat your offer, I shall gladly accept it, but if you feel the slightest hesitation about it, I shall not blame you for not renewing it."

And Robert told him everything, but Dudley declined to believe that there had been any just cause for the arrest, or that Robert had in any way violated the strictest canons of honor.

This young man seemed, indeed, to be perfect master of the art of making people believe in him in spite of the most damaging facts. Miss Sudie's faith in him never wavered for an instant. Even Billy had to keep a synopsis of the evidence against his cousin constantly in mind to keep himself from "believing that he couldn't see through glass," as he phrased it. The New York lawyer, summoned to get the young man out of jail, backed his faith in him, as we have seen, by indorsing his draft for several hundred dollars; and now Dudley, after hearing a plain statement of the facts from Robert's own lips, dismissed them as of no consequence, and set up his own unreasonable faith as a complete answer to them. He renewed his offer, and Robert accepted it, becoming office editor of the weekly paper for which he had recently been writing.

## CHAPTER XXVIII.

*Major Pagebrook asserts himself.*

IT now becomes necessary to a proper understanding of this history that we shall go back a day or two, to the day, in fact, on which Robert's letters were received at Shirley. I said there were three New York letters in the mail-bag thrown off at the Court House that morning. The third letter there referred to was from the law firm of Steel, Flint & Sharp. It was addressed to Edwin Pagebrook, Esq., and quite by accident it fell into that gentleman's hands. I say by accident, because Cousin Sarah Ann had taken unusual precautions to prevent precisely this result. After writing to the lawyers, it occurred to that estimable lady that a reply would come in due time, and that as she had taken the liberty of signing her husband's name to her letter, the reply would be addressed to him rather than to her, and she greatly feared that he would have an opportunity to read it. She particularly wished that this should not happen. She knew her mild-mannered and long-suffering husband thoroughly, and, while she felt free to torment him in various ways, she had learned, from one or two bits of experience, that it was not the part of wisdom to tax his endurance too far. Accordingly she took pains to prevent him from visiting the Court House while she was expecting the letter. She laid various plans for the purpose of keeping him occupied on the plantation every day, and took care to secure the first look into the family postbag whenever the servant returned with it. On the morning in question, however, as Maj. Pagebrook was riding over his plantation, inspecting work, he met a neighbor who was going to the Court House, and having some small matters to attend to there he determined to join the neighbor in his ride. Upon his arrival he called for his letters, and so it came about that the note in which Messrs. Steel, Flint & Sharp, "begged to inform him" of Robert's arrest in accordance with his instructions, fell into his hands. At first he was puzzled, and thought there must have been some mistake, but after awhile a glimmering of the truth dawned upon him, and in his smothered way he was exceedingly angry. He had condemned Robert's misconduct as severely as anybody, but had never dreamed of proceeding to harsh measures in the matter. Besides, it was only the day before that Robert's remittance of one hundred dollars had come to him, and, in acknowledging its receipt, he had partially satisfied his resentment by telling his cousin "what he thought of him," and to learn now that the young man was in jail for the fault, and apparently at his behest, was sorely displeasing to him. And worse than all, his wife had taken an unwarrantable liberty in the affair, and this he determined to resent. He mounted his horse, therefore, and was on the point of starting homeward when Dr. Harrison accosted him.

"Good morning, Maj. Pagebrook. May I speak to you a moment?"

"Good morning, Charles."

"Has there been any administrator appointed for Ewing's estate?"

"No, not yet. I reckon I must take out papers next court day, as he was of age when he died. It's only a matter of form, I reckon, as there are no debts."

"Well, my only reason for asking is I hold Ewing's note for two hundred and twenty-five dollars. I'm in no hurry, only I wanted to act regularly and get it in shape by presenting it."

"You have Ewing's note? Why, what is it for?" asked Major Pagebrook in astonishment.

"Borrowed money," answered the doctor.

"Borrowed money? But how did he come to borrow it?"

"Well, the fact is Ewing got to playing bluff with Foggy one day just before he got sick, and Foggy fleeced him pretty badly, and I lent him the money to pay out with. He didn't want to owe it to Foggy, you know."

"Have you the note with you?" asked Maj. Pagebrook.

"No. It's in my office; but I can get it if you'd like to look at it."

"No; it's no matter, if you can tell me the date."

"It bears date November 19th, I think."

"Just one day after he came of age," said Maj. Pagebrook.  "Well, I'll see about it, Charles," and with this the two gentlemen separated.

Major Pagebrook rode homeward, meditating upon the occurrences of the morning.  He had determined to manage his own business hereafter without tolerating improper interference upon the part of his wife, and he was in position to do this, too, except with regard to the home plantation, which, as Ewing had informed Robert, was held in Cousin Sarah Ann's name.  Major Pagebrook was a quiet man and a long-suffering one.  He liked nothing so much as peace, and to keep the peace he had always yielded to the more aggressive nature of his wife. But he felt now that the time had come for him to assert his supremacy in business matters, and he determined to assert it very quietly but very positively.  One point was as good as another, he thought, for the purpose, and this newly-discovered debt of Ewing's gave him an excellent occasion for the self-assertion upon which he had resolved.  Several times of late he had mildly suggested to Cousin Sarah Ann the propriety of putting Ewing's papers into Billy Barksdale's hands for examination, so that the boy's affairs might be properly and legally adjusted.  To every such suggestion Cousin Sarah Ann, who carried the key of Ewing's portable desk, had turned a deaf ear, saying that there were no debts one way or the other, and that she "wouldn't have anybody overhauling the poor boy's private papers."  Now, however, Major Pagebrook had made up his mind to put the desk into Billy's hands without asking the excellent lady's consent.

"Don't take my horse, Jim," he said to his servant upon arriving at home, "I am going to ride again presently. Just tie him to the rack till I want him."

Going into the house, he met Cousin Sarah Ann, to whom he said :

"Sarah Ann, I will write my own letters and attend to my own business hereafter, and I'll thank you not to sign my name for me again. You have placed me in a very awkward position, and I can't explain it to anybody without exposing you. Understand me now, please. I will not tolerate any such interference in future."

Ordinarily Cousin Sarah Ann would have been ready enough with a reply to such a remark as this, but just now she was fairly frightened by her husband's tone and manner. She saw at a glance that he was in very serious earnest, and she knew him well enough to know that it would not do to provoke him further. She was always afraid of him, even when she was riding rough-shod over him. When he seemed most submissive and she most aggressive, she was in the habit of scanning his countenance very carefully, as an engineer watches his steam gauge. When she saw steam rising, she usually had the safety valve—a flood of tears—ready for immediate use. Just now she saw indications of an explosion, which appalled her, and she dared not face the danger for a moment. Without reply, therefore, she sank, weeping, into the nearest chair, while her husband walked into her room, opened her wardrobe, and took from it the little desk in which his son's letters and papers were locked. Coming back to her he said :

"VERY WELL, THEN."

" I will take the key to this desk, if you please."

She looked up with a frightened countenance, and asked :

" What for ?"

" I want to open the desk."

" What are you going to do with it ?"

" I'm going to put it into my lawyer's hands."

" Wait then. I must look over the papers first."

" No ; Billy will do that."

" But there's some of mine in it, private ones."

" It doesn't matter. Billy will sort them and return yours to you."

" But he *sha'n't* look at my papers."

" Give me the key, Sarah Ann."

" I can't. It's lost."

" Very well then," said he, taking his knife from his pocket, breaking the frail lock, and walking out of the house without another word.

Cousin Sarah Ann was thoroughly overcome. She knew that her husband had received the reply to her letter, which she had meant to receive herself, and she knew too that her mastery over him was at an end, for the present at least. Worse than all, she knew that the desk and its contents would inevitably go into Billy Barksdale's hands, and she had her own reasons for thinking this the sorest affliction possible to her. There was no help for it now, however, and she could do nothing except throw herself on her bed and shed tears of bitter mortification, vexation, and dread.

Meanwhile Major Pagebrook galloped over to Shirley,

with the desk under his arm. The conversation already reported between Billy and Miss Sudie, was hardly more than finished when he dismounted and walked into the young lawyer's office.

He opened his business by telling Billy about the note held by Dr. Harrison.

"I don't understand it," he said. "Harrison says the note is dated November 19th, which was just one day after Ewing came of age, and I remember that Ewing was taken sick on the morning of his birthday—very sick, as you know, and never left his bed afterwards."

"When was Ewing at the Court House last?" asked Billy.

"Not since the day Robert left."

"Did he owe Harrison any money that you know of?"

"No; but Harrison says Foggy won that much from him, and he had to borrow to pay it."

"You are sure, however, that Ewing could not possibly have had a chance to sign the note after he came of age?"

"Of course he couldn't. He was delirious from the very first, and we never left him."

"I think I see how it is," said Billy. "Foggy and Charley Harrison are too intimate for any straight dealings. I reckon Charley was as deeply interested in the winnings as Foggy was, but they have made Ewing execute the note to Charley for money borrowed to pay Foggy with so that it would be legally good. They made him date it ahead, too, so that it would appear to have been executed after Ewing came of age. They didn't anticipate his sickness, and they haven't thought to compare dates. I think we can beat them this time, when they get ready to sue."

"But we mustn't let them sue, Billy," said Major Pagebrook. "I would never consent to plead the baby act or to get out of it by any legal quibble if the signature is genuine, as I reckon it is. That wouldn't be honorable. No, I shall pay the note off; and I only want to know whether I must charge it to Ewing's estate or not, after taking out administration papers. If I can, I ought to, in justice to the other children. If I. can't, I must pay it myself. Look into it, please, and let me know about it. I have brought you Ewing's desk, so you can look over all his papers and attend to all his affairs for me. I want to get everything straight." So saying he took his leave.

# CHAPTER XXIX.

*Mr. Barksdale, the Younger, Goes upon a Journey.*

NOT until the next morning did Mr. Billy find time to examine the papers in Ewing's desk. Indeed, even then he deemed the matter one of very little consequence, inasmuch as the papers, whatever they might happen to be, were probably of no legal importance, being of necessity the work of a minor. There might be memoranda there, however, and possibly a will disposing of personal property, which, under the law of Virginia, would be good if executed by a minor over eighteen years of age.

In view of these possibilities, therefore, Billy sat down to the task of examining the papers, which were pretty numerous, such as they were. After awhile he became interested in the very miscellaneousness of the assortment. Little memoranda were there—of the date on which a horse had been shod; of the amount paid for a new pair of boots; of the times at which the boy had written letters to his friends, and of a hundred other unimportant things. There were bits of poor verse, too, such as may be found in the desk of almost every boy.

Old letters, full of nothing, were there in abundance, but nothing which could possibly be of any value to anybody. On all the letters, except one, was marked, in Ewing's handwriting, "To be burned without reading, in case of my death." The one exception attracted Billy's attention, and opening it, he was surprised to find Robert Pagebrook's name appended to it. It was, in fact, the letter which Cousin Sarah Ann had opened during her son's last illness. After reading it Mr. Billy sat down to think. Presently, looking at his watch, he went to the door and called a servant.

"Go and ask your Miss Sudie to put two or three shirts, and some socks and handkerchiefs into my satchel for me, and then you go and tell Polidore to saddle Graybeard and the bay, and get ready to go with me to the Court House directly. Do you hear?"

The servant made no answer to the question with which Mr. Billy closed his speech. Indeed that gentleman expected none. Virginians always ask "do you hear?" when they give instructions to servants, and they never get or expect an answer. Without the question, however, they would never secure attention to the instruction. To say, "do so and so," without adding, "do you hear?" would be the idlest possible waste of words on the part of any one giving an order to the average Virginian house servant.

Mr. Billy was in the habit of making sudden journeys on business, without giving the slightest warning to the family except that contained in a request that his satchel or saddle-bags be packed, so that Miss Sudie was not in

the least surprised when his present message came to her.
She was surprised, however, when, instead of riding
away without a word of farewell, as he usually did, he
came into the house, and, kissing her tenderly, said :

"Keep your spirits up, Sudie, and don't let things
worry you too much. I'm going to Richmond on the two
o'clock train, and don't know how long I'll be gone.
Good-by, little girl," and he kissed her again. All
this was quite out of character, Miss Sudie felt. Billy
was affectionate enough, at all times, but he detested
leave-takings, and always avoided them when he could.
To seek one was quite unlike him, and Miss Sudie was
puzzled to know what prompted him to do it on this particular occasion. He rode away, however, without offering any explanation whatever.

Mr. Billy went to Richmond, as he had said he intended doing, but he did not remain there an hour. He
went to the cashier of a bank, a gentleman with whom
he was well acquainted, got from him a letter of introduction to a prominent man in Philadelphia, and left for
that city on the first train.

Arriving in Philadelphia about nine o'clock the next
day, Mr. Billy ate a hasty breakfast and proceeded to
the little collegiate institute in which Robert had once
been a professor, as the reader will remember. Intro-
ducing himself to President Currier he asked for a
private interview, and was invited for the purpose into
Dr. Currier's inner office.

"I believe, doctor," he said, after telling that gentleman
who he was, "that there was something due Professor

Pagebrook on his salary at the time his connection with this college terminated, was there not?"

"Yes, sir; there was about three hundred dollars due him, if I remember correctly, but it has been paid, I think."

"Have you any way of ascertaining precisely how and when?" asked Billy.

"Yes; my own letter-book should show. Let me see," turning over the leaves, "Ah, here it is. A draft for the amount was sent to him by letter on the eighth of November, addressed to —— Court House, Virginia."

"Thank you," said Billy. "The draft, I suppose, was regular New York Exchange?"

"Of course."

"Would you mind telling me from what bank you bought it, and to whose order, in the first place, it was made payable? Pardon my asking such questions, but I need this information for use in the cause of justice."

"O you need offer no apology, I assure you, sir," returned the president. "I have nothing to conceal in the matter. The draft was drawn by the Susquehanna Bank, and to my order, I think. Yes, I remember indorsing it."

"Thank you, sir," said Billy. "You are very courteous, and I am indebted to you for information which I should have found it difficult to get from any other source. Good morning, sir."

Leaving the college, which was situated in one of the suburbs, Mr. Billy took a carriage and drove into the city. There he delivered his letter of introduction, and secured from the gentleman to whom it was addressed a personal introduction to the cashier of the Susquehanna Bank. To this latter person he said :

"I am looking up evidence in a case, and, if I am not greatly mistaken, you can help me in an effort to set a wrong right. On the eighth of last month you sold a draft on New York for three hundred dollars, payable to the order of David Currier. Now, in the ordinary course of business I suppose that draft has been returned to you after payment."

"Yes, if it was paid before the first of the month. We settle with our New York correspondents once a month. I'll look at the last batch of returned checks and see."

"Thank you. I should be glad to see the indorsements on the paper, if possible."

The cashier went to the vault, and returning with a large bundle of canceled checks soon found the one wanted. Billy turned it over and examined the indorsements on the back. Then, turning to the banker, he asked :

"Would it be possible for me to get temporary possession of this draft by depositing the amount of its face with you until its return ?"

"You merely wish it for use in evidence ?" asked the banker.

"That's all," said Billy.

"You can take it, then, without a deposit, Mr. Barksdale. It is of no value now, but we usually keep our canceled exchange, so I shall be obliged if you will return this when you've done with it."

This was precisely what Robert had come to Philadelphia to secure, and after finding what the indorsements on the draft were, he would willingly have paid its face outright, if that had been necessary, to get possession of it.

Who knows what the value of a bit of writing may be, even after its purpose has to all appearance been fully answered? I know a great commercial house in which it is an inexorable law that no bit of paper once written on in the way of business shall ever be destroyed, however valueless it may seem to be; and on more than one occasion the wisdom of the rule has been strikingly made manifest. So it was with this paid, canceled, and returned draft. Worthless in all eyes but his, to Billy it was far more precious than if it had been crisp and new, and payable to his own order.

## CHAPTER XXX.

*The younger Mr. Barksdale Asks to be put upon His Oath.*

IT was nearly noon when the train which brought Billy Barksdale back from Philadelphia stopped at the Court House, and that young gentleman went from the station immediately to the court room, where the Circuit Court, as he knew, was in session.

"Has the grand jury been impaneled yet?" he asked the commonwealth's attorney.

"Yes; it has just gone out, but as usual there is nothing for it to do, so it will report 'no bills' in an hour or so, I reckon."

"Have me sworn and sent before it then," said Billy. "I think I can put it in the way of finding something to do."

The official was astonished, but he lost no time in complying with the rather singular request. Billy went before the grand jury, and remained there for a considerable time. This was a very unusual occurrence in every way, and it quickly produced a buzz of excitement in and about the building. There was rarely ever anything for grand juries to do in this quiet county, and when there was anything it usually hinged upon some publicly known and talked of matter. Everybody knew in advance what it was about, and the probable result was easy to predict. Now, however, all was mystery. A prominent young lawyer had been sworn and sent before the grand jury at his own request, and the length of time during which he was detained there effectually dispelled the belief which at first obtained, that he merely wanted to secure the presentment of some negligent road overseer. Even the commonwealth's attorney could not manage to look wise enough, as he sat there stroking his beard, to deceive anybody into the belief that he knew what was going on. The minutes were very long ones. The excitement soon extended beyond the court house, and everybody in the village was on tiptoe with suppressed curiosity. The court room was full to overflowing when Billy came quietly out of the grand jury's apartment and took his seat in the bar as if nothing out of the ordinary course of affairs had happened.

It did not tend to allay the excitement, certainly, when the deputy sheriff on duty at the door of the jury room beckoned to the commonwealth's attorney and that gentleman went up-stairs three steps at a time, disappearing within the chamber devoted to the secret inquest and remaining there. When half an hour later Major Edwin Pagebrook was called, sworn and sent up as a witness, wild rumors of a secret crime among the better classes began to circulate freely in the crowd, starting from nowhere and gradually taking definite shape as they spread from one to another of the eager villagers·

The excitement was now absolutely painful in its intensity, and even the judge himself began walking restlessly back and forth in the space set apart for the bench.

When Major Pagebrook came out of the room with a downcast face he went immediately home, and Rosenwater, a merchant in the village, was called. When he came out, distinct efforts were made to worm the secret from him. He was mindful of his oath, however, and refused to say anything.

Finally the members of the grand jury marched slowly down stairs, and took their stand in front of the clerk's desk.

"Poll the grand jury," said the judge. When that ceremony was over, the question which everybody in the building had been mentally asking for hours was formulated by the court.

"Gentlemen of the grand jury, have you any presentments to make?"

"We have, your honor," answered the foreman.

"Read the report of the grand jury, Mr. Clerk."

The official rose and after adjusting his spectacles very deliberately, read aloud :

"We, the grand jury, on our oaths present Dr. Charles Harrison and James Madison Raves, for forgery and for a conspiracy to defraud Edwin Pagebrook, on or about the tenth day of November in this present year within the jurisdiction of this honorable court."

The crowd was fairly stunned. Nobody knew or could guess what it meant. The commonwealth's attorney was the first to speak.

"As the legal representative of the commonwealth, I move the court to issue a warrant for the arrest of Charles Harrison and James Madison Raves, and I ask that the grand jury be instructed to return to their room and to put their indictments in proper form."

The two men thus accused of crime being present in court were taken in charge by the sheriff.

"If the commonwealth's attorney has no further motions to make in this case," said the judge, "the court will take a recess, in order to give time for the preparation of indictments in due form."

"May it please the court," said the official addressed, "I have only to ask that your honor will instruct the sheriff to separate the two prisoners during the recess. I do not know that this is necessary, but it may tend to further the interests of justice."

"The court sees no reason to refuse the request," said the judge. "Mr. Sheriff, you will see that your two prisoners are not allowed to confer together in any way until after the reassembling of the court, at four o'clock."

## CHAPTER XXXI.

*Mr. William Barksdale Explains.*

PRECISELY what Dr. Harrison's emotions were when he found himself in the sheriff's hands, nobody is likely ever to know, as that gentleman was always of taciturn mood in matters closely concerning himself, and on the present occasion was literally dumb.

With Foggy the case was different. He was always a prudent man. He was not given to the taking of unnecessary risks for the sake of abstract principles. He made no pretensions to the possession of heroic fortitude under affliction, and he had no special reputation for high-toned honor to lose. The clutch of the law was to him an uncomfortable one, and he was prepared to escape it by any route which might happen to be open to him. This disposition upon his part was an important factor in the problem which Billy had set out to solve. He knew Foggy was a moral coward, and upon his cowardice he depended, in part, for the success of his undertaking.

As soon as court adjourned the commonwealth's attorney requested the members of the grand jury to make themselves as comfortable as might be while he should be engaged in the preparation of formal indictments against the two prisoners. Going then to his office he closeted himself with Billy Barksdale, who had preceded him thither by his request.

"You'll help me with this prosecution, won't you Billy?" he asked.

"With as good a will as I ever carried to a fish fry," said Billy.

"Well, then," said the attorney, "tell me just how the thing stands. I confess I'm all in a jumble about it. Begin at the beginning and tell the whole story. Then we'll know where we stand and how to proceed."

Accordingly Billy recounted the history of the protested draft; the promise to pay; its nonfulfillment and the trouble which ensued. He then continued:

"My suspicions as to the real facts of the case were aroused by accident. Maj. Pagebrook consulted me a few days ago about a note signed by Ewing Pagebrook, drawn in favor of Charley Harrison, which, Harrison said, had been given him when he advanced money to Ewing with which to pay a gambling debt to Foggy. That note was evidently dated ahead, as it bore date of November 19th, one day after Ewing attained his majority, when, in fact, the boy was taken ill on the morning of his twenty-first birthday, and never left his bed afterwards. This confirmed me in the belief that Foggy and Harrison were confederates in their gambling operations. They fleeced the boy, and then had him borrow the money with which to pay from Harrison, and give a note for it, so as to

make the consideration good ; and they took pains to
have him date it ahead, so as to get rid of the minority
trouble.  This by itself would have amounted to nothing,
but in looking over Ewing's papers I found a letter there
from Bob Pagebrook, which I happened accidentally to
know was received during Ewing's illness.  Here it is.  I'll
read it.

"'MY DEAR EWING :—I can not tell you how grieved
I am at the news your letter brings me.  I can ill afford
to lose the three hundred dollars which I intrusted to
you to hand to your father, and even if you do make it
good when you come of age, as you so solemnly promise
me you will, I am, meanwhile, placed in a very awkward
position with regard to it.  I promised your father to pay
him that money by a certain day, and was greatly pleased,
as you know, when, upon arriving at the Court House on
my way north, I found the remittance awaiting me there,
as it enabled me to make the payment in advance of the
time agreed upon.  When I, in my haste to catch the
train, gave you the check to give to your father, I dismissed the subject from my mind, and set about the
work of repairing my fortunes with a light heart, little
thinking that matters would turn out as they have.

"'But while I am sorely annoyed by the fact that this
may place me in an awkward position, I am willing to
trust my reputation in your hands.  Remember that you
are now bound in honor, not merely to pay this money as
soon as you shall attain your majority, but also to protect
me from undeserved disgrace by frankly stating the facts
of the case to your father in the event of his entertain-

ing doubts of my integrity. This much you are in honor bound to do in any case, and you have also given me your word that you will do it. If your father shall seem disposed to think me not unduly dilatory in the matter of payment, you need tell him nothing. You may spare yourself that mortification, · send me the money, and I will remit it to him, merely saying that unavoidable circumstances which I am not at liberty to explain have prevented the earlier payment which I intended to make.

" 'But in agreeing to do this, Ewing, I am moved solely by my desire to shield you from disgrace and consequent ruin. When I gave you that money for your father it was a sacred trust, and in converting it to other uses you not only wronged me, but you made yourself guilty of something very like a crime. Pardon me if I speak plainly, for I am speaking only for your good and I speak only to you. I want you to understand how terribly wrong and altogether dishonorable your act was, so that you may never be guilty of another such. I am not disposed to reproach you, but I do want to warn you. You are the son of a gentleman, and you have no right to bring disgrace upon your father's name. You ought not to gamble, and if you do gamble you have no right to surrender your honor in payment of your losses. I promise you, as you ask me to do, that I will not tell what you have done ; and you know I never break a promise under any circumstances whatever. But in promising this I place my own reputation in your keeping, depending upon you, in the event of necessity, to frankly acknowledge your fault, so that I may not

appear to have run away from a debt which in **fact I**
have paid.'

"When I read that letter," continued Billy, "I began
to see daylight. Bob had given his word of honor to
Ewing not to expose him. Ewing had died before he
could make the money matter good, and Bob, like the
great, big, honorable, dear old fellow that he is, allowed
himself to go to jail and bear the reputation of an absconding debtor, rather than break his promise to the
dead boy. He paid the money again, too. I suspected,
of course, that Foggy and Charley Harrison were mixed
up in the matter some way, particularly as the very last
visit Ewing ever made to the Court House was made on
the day that Bob went away. I went to Philadelphia, and there found the canceled draft, drawn in
favor of David Currier ; indorsed to Robert Pagebrook ;
and by him indorsed to Edwin Pagebrook. Then followed, as you know, an indorsement to James M. Raves,
signed 'E. Pagebrook.' That, of course, was written by
Ewing, who at the suggestion of these two men made
the draft over to them—or to one of them—by signing
his own name, which happened, when written with the
initial only, to be the same as his father's. Foggy then
indorsed it to Harrison, and he, being respectable, had
no difficulty in getting Rosenwater to cash it for him.
It never entered Rosenwater's head, of course, to question any of the signatures back of Harrison's. Now my
theory is that this draft did not cover Ewing's losses by
two hundred and twenty-five dollars ; and so the two
thrifty gentlemen made the boy execute the note that

Harrison holds for that amount, dating it ahead, and making it for borrowed money."

"You're right, Barksdale, without a doubt," said the commonwealth's attorney; "but how are we going to make a jury see it? There's plenty of evidence to found an indictment on, but I'm afraid there a'n't enough to secure a conviction."

"That's true," said Billy. "But we must do our very best. If we can't convict both, we may one; and even if we fail altogether in the prosecution, we will at least expose the rascals, and this county will be too hot for them afterwards. Foggy is always shaky in the knees, and if we give him half a chance will turn state's evidence. Why not sound him on the subject?"

Foggy needed very little sounding indeed. At the first intimation that there might be hope for him if he would tell what he knew he volunteered a confession, which bore out Billy's theory to the letter. From his statement, too, it appeared that Harrison was the author of the whole scheme. He had overborne Ewing's scruples, and by dint of threats compelled him to commit a practical forgery by writing his own name in such a way as to make it appear to be his father's. While Foggy was at it he made a clean breast, telling all about his partnership with Harrison in the gambling operations, and admitting that the note Harrison held was dated ahead and given solely for a gambling debt.

The commonwealth's attorney agreed to enter a *nolle prosequi* in Foggy's case, and to transfer him, at the trial, from the prisoner's box to the witness stand.

When Billy came out from this conference he found Major Pagebrook awaiting an opportunity to speak to him. The major, it seems, after going home had returned to the Court House.

"Billy," he said, "I know now about that letter from Robert to Ewing. Sarah Ann has told me she read it when it came. What is to be done about it?"

"Nothing," said Billy, "except that you will of course return Robert the extra three hundred dollars he has paid you."

"Of course I'll do that. But I mean—the fact is I don't want that letter to appear on the trial. You will have to tell where you got it, and it will come out, in spite of everything, that Sarah Ann knew of it."

"Well, Cousin Edwin, what am I to do? This has been a wretched business from first to last. Poor Bob has suffered severely for Ewing's fault, and—I must speak plainly—through Cous—through your wife's iniquity. Not only has he had to pay the money twice, he has been sent to jail, and but for a lucky accident his reputation as an honorable man would have been destroyed forever, and that merely to gratify your wife's petty and unreasonable spite against him. It became my duty to unravel this mystery for the sake of freeing Bob from an unjust and undeserved disgrace. In doing that I have accidentally stumbled upon the discovery of a crime, and even if it were not illegal I am not the man to compound a felony. For you I am heartily sorry, but your wife is only reaping what she has sown. I would do anything honorable to spare your feelings, Cousin Edwin, but I can not help giving evidence in this case. I really do not see, however, precisely how Bob's letter can be used as evidence. If it had been sufficient in itself to establish the facts to which it referred I should have used it to set Bob right, and the thing would have ended there. But Bob's statement was of course an interested one, and I feared that after a time, if not immediately, gossip would seize upon that point and say the whole thing was made up merely to clear Bob. I knew he would never show Ewing's letter to which his was a reply, and so I set myself to work hunting up the draft. I don't see how the letter can well come up on the trial, but if it should become necessary for me to tell about it, I must tell all about it, of course."

Major Pagebrook walked away, his head bowed as if there were a heavy weight upon his shoulders, and Billy pitied him heartily. This woman, who, in her groundless malignity, had wrought so much wrong and brought so much of sorrow upon the good old man, was his wife, and he could not free himself from the fact or its consequences. He had never willingly done a wrong in his life, and it seemed peculiarly hard that he should now have to suffer so sorely for the sins of the woman whom he called wife.

## CHAPTER XXXII.

### *Which Is also The Last.*

UPON leaving Major Pagebrook Billy mounted his horse and galloped away toward Shirley, not caring to remain till the court should reassemble at four, as there could hardly be any business done beyond the formal presentation of the indictments by the grand jury and the committal of the prisoners to await trial.

When he entered the yard gate at Shirley he found his father, who had returned from the court house some time before, awaiting him.

"I have not told Sudie, my son," said the old gentleman. "I found it hard to keep my lips closed, but you have managed this affair grandly, my boy, and you ought to have the pleasure of telling the story in your own way. Go into the office, and I'll send Sudie to you."

Miss Sudie was naturally enough alarmed when her uncle, repressing everything like an expression of joy, and in doing that managing to look as solemn as a death warrant, told her that Billy wanted to see her in the office immediately. But Billy's look, as she entered, reassured her. He met her just inside the door, and taking her face between his hands, said :

"I'M AS PROUD AND AS GLAD AS A BOY WITH RED MOROCCO TOPS TO
HIS BOOTS."

"I'm as proud and as glad as a boy with red morocco tops to his boots, little girl."

"What about, Cousin Billy?" asked Miss Sudie in a tremor of uncertainty.

"Because I've been doing the duty you set me. I've been 'turning something up.' I've torn the mask off of that dear old rascal Bob Pagebrook, and shown him up in his true colors. It's just shameful the way he's been deceiving us, making us think him an absconding debtor and all that when he a'n't anything of the sort. He's as true as—as you are. There; that's a figure of speech he'd approve if he could hear it, and he shall too. I'm going to write him a letter to-night, telling him just what I think of him."

There was a little flutter in Miss Sudie's manner as she sat down, unable to stand any longer.

"Tell me about it, please," was all she could say.

"Well, in a word, Bob's all right, with a big balance over. He's as straight as a well rope when the bucket's full. Let me make you understand that in advance, and then I'll tell my story."

And with this Billy proceeded in his own way to tell the young woman all about the visit to Philadelphia and its results. When he had finished Miss Sudie simply sat and looked at him, smiling through her tears the thankfulness she could not put into words. When after awhile she found her voice she said some things which were very pleasant indeed to Mr. Billy in the hearing.

The next day's mail carried three letters to Mr. Robert Pagebrook. What Miss Sudie said in hers I do not know,

and if I did I should not tell.   Col. Barksdale wrote in a
stately way, as he always did when he meant to be particularly affectionate, the gist of his letter lying in the
sentence with which he opened it, which was :

"I did not know, until now, how much of your father
there is in you."

Mr. Billy's letter would make the fortune of any comic
paper if it could be published.   Robert insists that there
were just three hundred and sixty-five hitherto unheard
of metaphors in the body of it, and twenty-one more in
the postscript.   He says he counted them carefully.

Naturally enough, after all that had happened, everybody at Shirley wanted Robert to come back again as
soon as possible, and one and all entreated him to spend
the Christmas there.   This he promised to do, but at the
last moment he was forced to abandon his purpose in
consequence of the utter failure of Mr. Dudley's health,
an occurrence which left Robert with the entire burden
of the paper upon him, and made it impossible for him to
leave New York during the holidays.   Even with Robert
there the publishers were anxious about the management
of the paper at so critical a time ; but Robert's single-
handed success fully justified the confidence Mr. Dudley
had felt and expressed in his ability to conduct the
paper, and when, a month later, Dudley resigned entirely, to go abroad in search of health, our friend Robert
Pagebrook was promoted to his place and pay, having
won his way in a few months to a position in his new
profession which he had not hoped to gain without
years of patient toil.

The rest of my story hardly needs telling. The winter was passed in hard work on Robert's part, but the work was of a sort which it delighted him to do. He knew the worth of printed words, and rejoiced in the possession of that power which the printing-press only can give to a man, multiplying him, as it were, and enabling him to give utterance to his thought in the presence of an audience too vast and too widely scattered ever to be reached by any one human voice. It was a favorite theory of his, too, that printed words carry with them some of the force expended upon them by the press itself—that a sentence which would fall meaningless from its author's lips may mold a score of human lives if it be put in type. He was and is an enthusiast in his work, and never apostle went forth to preach a new gospel with more of earnestness or with a stronger sense of responsibility than Robert Pagebrook brings with him daily to his desk.

The winter softened into spring, and when the spring was richest in its promise there was a quiet wedding at Shirley.

My story is fully told, but my friend who writes novels insists that I must not lay down the pen until I shall have gathered up what he calls the loose threads, and knitted them into a seemly and unraveled end.

Major Pagebrook, dreading the possible exposure of his wife's misconduct, placed money in the hands of a friend, and that friend became surety for Dr. Harrison's appearance when called for trial. Of course Dr. Harrison betook himself to other parts, going, indeed, to the West Indies, where he died of yellow fever a year or two later. Foggy disappeared also, but whither he went I really do not know.

Billy Barksdale is still a bachelor, and still likes to listen while Aunt Catherine explains relationships with her keys.

Col. Barksdale has retired from practice, and lives quietly at Shirley.

Cousin Sarah Ann is still Cousin Sarah Ann, but she lives in Richmond now, having discovered years ago that the air of the country did not agree with her.

Robert and Sudie have a pretty little place in the country, within half an hour's ride of New York, and I sometimes run out to spend a quiet Sunday with Cousin Sudie. Robert I can see in his office any day. Their oldest boy, William Barksdale Pagebrook, entered college last September.

# THE
# Hoosier School-Master.

## By EDWARD EGGLESTON.

⧫ ◆ ⧫

### Finely Illustrated, with 12 full-page Engravings and Numerous other Cuts.

⧫ ◆ ⧫

## CONTENTS.

### Price, post-paid, $1.25.

# ORANGE JUDD & COMPANY,
## 245 BROADWAY, NEW-YORK.

# THE
# END OF THE WORLD.

## A LOVE STORY.

BY

## EDWARD EGGLESTON,

Author of "The Hoosier School-master," etc.

— ◆ ◆ ◆ —

**With 15 full page Engravings, and numerous other Fine Illustrations.**

— ◆ ◆ ◆ —

# CONTENTS.

— ◆ —

**PRICE, Post-paid, $1.50.**

— ◆ —

# ORANGE JUDD & COMPANY,

*245 Broadway, New-York.*

# THE MYSTERY

OF

# METROPOLISVILLE.

## By EDWARD EGGLESTON,

*Author of "The Hoosier School-Master," "The End of the World,"
etc.*

### With Thirteen Illustrations.

——◇——

## CONTENTS.

## ILLUSTRATIONS.—By FRANK BEARD.

### PRICE, POST-PAID, $1.50.

## ORANGE JUDD & COMPANY,

### 245 Broadway, New-York.

# PRACTICAL FLORICULTURE;

## A Guide to the Successful Propagation and Cultivation

OF

# FLORISTS' PLANTS.

## By PETER HENDERSON, BERGEN CITY, N. J.,

AUTHOR OF "GARDENING FOR PROFIT."

————— ◆◆◆ —————

MR. HENDERSON is known as the largest Commercial Florist in the country. In the present work he gives a full account of his modes of propagation and cultivation. It is adapted to the wants of the amateur, as well as the professional grower.

The scope of the work may be judged from the following

## TABLE OF CONTENTS.

Beautifully Illustrated. Sent post-paid. Price, $1.50.

## ORANGE JUDD & CO.,

### 245 Broadway New-York.

# PARSONS ON THE ROSE.

## A TREATISE ON THE

## Propagation, Culture, and History of the Rose.

### By SAMUEL B. PARSONS.

## NEW AND REVISED EDITION.

### ILLUSTRATED.

———

THE Rose is the only flower that can be said to have a history. It is popular now, and was so centuries ago. In his work upon the Rose, Mr. Parsons has gathered up the curious legends concerning the flower, and gives us an idea of the esteem in which it was held in former times. A simple garden classification has been adopted, and the leading varieties under each class enumerated and briefly described. The chapters on multiplication, cultivation, and training, are very full, and the work is altogether the most complete of any before the public.

The following is from the author's Preface:

"In offering a new edition of this work, the preparation of which gave us pleasure more than twenty years ago, we have not only carefully revised the garden classification, but have stricken out much of the poetry, which, to the cultivator, may have seemed irrelevant, if not worthless. For the interest of the classical scholar, we have retained much of the early history of the Rose, and its connection with the manners and customs of the two great nations of a former age.

"The amateur will, we think, find the labor of selection much diminished by the increased simplicity of the mode we have adopted, while the commercial gardener will in nowise be injured by the change.

"In directions for culture, we give the results of our own experience, and have not hesitated to avail ourselves of any satisfactory results in the experience of others, which might enhance the utility of the work."

———

## CONTENTS:

PRICE, POST-PAID $1.50.

## ORANGE JUDD & CO.,

### 245 Broadway, New-York.

www.ingramcontent.com/pod-product-compliance
Lightning Source LLC
Chambersburg PA
CBHW030118030726
47498CB00007B/2442